A Surgeon's Miracle

By Ludima Gus Burton

PublishAmerica
Baltimore

ISBN: 1-4241-7378-7
PUBLISHED BY PUBLISHAMERICA, LLLP
www.publishamerica.com
Baltimore

Printed in the United States of America

Dedicated to my sister, Leona Dubay,
for her love, encouragement and belief in my efforts
and
to the memory of my brother, William Wanic, who,
with the others in the CCC (Civilian Conservation Corps),
made our parks beautiful forever.

Prologue

The plastic surgeon had performed a miracle.

Her fingers gripped the hand mirror. Each day she forced herself to look at her face.

Wide blue eyes, fringed with thick lashes, stared at her from under thin black eyebrows. Pink skin glowed over high cheekbones. A straight nose. A dimple appeared in her left cheek when she forced a smile. A square chin gave her a look of determination. Her short black hair, cropped straight across, covered small ears.

A beautiful face.

Yet, was it truly hers? Surely she had remembered what she looked like before the accident. Had even given directions—but, now, she wasn't so certain.

Well, it was done.

Chapter 1

"Hey, Cassie's here!"

The message echoed to all parts of the Silver Spur Stable located a few miles outside of Hawthorne in Upstate New York. The slanting rays of the setting sun made patterns on the floor. A May breeze stirred the sawdust.

Kyle Chandler looked toward the barn door. When Cassandra Brown came through the wide doorway holding a large container filled with cookies, a low whistle crept past his lips.

The sight of her in faded, fitted blue jeans, clinging like skin to her slim hips and long thighs, took his breath away. Western boots tapped an uneven beat on the cement floor. The silver studs on her sky blue shirt glittered. He smiled at the large Stetson she wore at the back of her head.

Today she was a far cry from the project manager he summoned to a board meeting yesterday morning to be introduced to the new CEO of the Spencer headquarters of the Chandler Corporation. Then, a black tailored suit made her blend in with all the others present.

Earlier, when familiarizing himself with his department heads, the name Brown had thrown him for a heartbeat. His ex-wife Colleen's maiden name had been Brown. A quick perusal of Cassandra's personnel file banished any connection. Just a common name. That was all. Still, the coincidence had been unnerving.

When she answered his questions about her department, Cassandra's soft, husky voice lingered in his memory. As had the disturbing limp that marred her perfection when she walked out of the room.

The tall stable hands soon surrounded Cassie, hiding her from Kyle's view.

"Hey," Gary Madison called to her. "Leave a couple for Kyle and me." He turned to Kyle. "Cassie makes great cookies for us every Saturday. I hope it's chocolate chip this week."

Kyle lagged behind Gary. He and Gary had come in from a trail ride. In the last few weeks they had renewed an old college friendship. Kyle reached for his cookie, his gaze locking on Cassie's startled blue eyes.

"This is a surprise, Miss Brown."

Her slow smile grew into such a radiant one that his pulse leaped. The container of cookies in her hand shook. He reached out to steady it and closed his hand over hers. The shock of the contact jolted him. She quickly stepped away from him.

Her remembered voice was low. "Excuse me. I have to see Harry and give him his."

Kyle watched her limp into the shadows of the barn, a sensual sway to her hips. He looked up to see Gary observing him, a quizzical look on his face.

"She's lovely, isn't she?" Kyle said, a sheepish smile curving his lips. "She works for my company."

"I know. I'm the one who helped her apply there."

"I met her yesterday at my board meeting."

Kyle said no more. He didn't want Gary to think he had an

interest in Cassie. Besides, it would go no further. He had moved his corporate office to Spencer to get away from his unhappy past. A relationship with any woman wasn't for him.

Cassie didn't leave the sanctuary of the stables until she saw the two men drive away. Her heart stopped its racing and her hands, their trembling. To meet her employer on her home territory disturbed her. To see that Gary and he appeared to be close friends also upset her.

Would Kyle Chandler, her boss, come to the stable every weekend? If so, she'd make herself scarce. She didn't understand why her heartbeat quickened or her mouth became dry when he came near her.

Naturally, the whole office had been interested in what was going to happen with a new CEO. Never mind that he was handsome—six feet tall with streaked blond hair. His broad shoulders communicated power and presence. His eyes were dark brown instead of her expected blue. When he spoke to his employees, he had been brisk and authoritative. The introductory meeting was reassuring to all of the employees.

During the following week she didn't meet or even see Kyle Chandler. She wondered why a feeling of disappointment colored her days.

Looking forward to the weekend, she took her bus to Hawthorne on Friday afternoon. Having her own car would have been more convenient, but her accident had left her afraid to drive. She knew she should conquer this fear but kept putting it off. The bus was fine.

When the main street of Hawthorne came into view, Cassie breathed a sigh of pleasure. She felt happy and safe living here. The fear of an unknown man that she had felt when she came out of her amnesia rarely surfaced now.

Her hip throbbed. She walked slowly to her apartment. She wondered that she held on to the limp and kept putting off the operation. Surely she could take the pain again.

What did Kyle Chandler think? Was she repulsive to him? She

had seen the way the limp had affected some would-be admirers. She wanted to be liked and loved for herself. No operation at this time. Never mind what Kyle Chandler thought.

Exasperation filled her. She'd done it again, thinking of the man who probably wouldn't give her a second thought.

On reaching her apartment, she stirred the ingredients for the oatmeal cookies she'd bake for the Silver Spur Stable hands. The weekly cookies had become her thanks to them for saving her life. She'd never forget them.

With the cookies cooling on the racks, Cassie went for her walk. The day slowly slipped into a soft twilight with the vivid green grass as the last color to disappear into the blue of the night.

At the end of Featherstone Lane stood the house of her dreams. A big, rambling house with weathered shingles, missing shutters and in need of much repair. Along a stone wall, however, daffodils and a lone red tulip struggled to reveal that this had once been a tended flower garden.

A faded FOR SALE sign was almost buried in the surrounding weeds. No one but she wanted it. Only she didn't have the money to buy it. She gave a deep sigh and returned to her apartment.

Saturday morning Kyle and Gary drove into the parking lot at the stable for their trail ride. Back home in Broderick Kyle had ridden on a regular basis. It was good to be here. He looked around. He liked the village with its tree-lined streets, the old houses, the flower gardens and the small business section. The overall peace and quiet of a good life swept over him. It might be the place to put down roots.

On the trail ride, Gary and Kyle stopped at the top of a hill. They admired the majestic sweep from the rugged cliffs to the valley below.

"I'm glad I moved away from Broderick," Kyle said. "As I look back, I realize, more and more, that I let my business become more important than my wife's happiness."

"Have you heard from Colleen since she left?"

"No. For a time, I had an investigator looking. She, evidently, doesn't want to come back. It's been two years. I've finally accepted her decision by her silence. It would be good to actually hear from her. This isn't like her at all. She was always so thoughtful."

Gary saw the lines of suffering etched around Kyle's eyes and the bleak look in them.

"This has been a hard time for you," he said.

Kyle shrugged his shoulders. "I'm making a new life for myself. Hawthorne's a good place to start." He gave a short laugh. "Think I'll buy a house here. Know of any available?"

"As a matter of fact, I do. I'll take you tomorrow, if you like."

"Sure thing."

As they rode back Kyle wondered what Cassie Brown would think of him living in her village. And why was he thinking of her any way? Last week he pulled out her file and was pleased with her efficiency and competence as a project manager. And found himself recalling her several times during the day. Her lovely face haunted him. Her elusive dimple kept nagging him. When she smiled at him at the stable he was taken aback for a minute. Colleen's remembered dimple flashed before him—as well as her slightly turned up nose and round chin. No way could he mistake Cassie's features and voice with his wife. He breathed a sigh of relief. He was too sensible to be fooled this way.

The next morning Gary and Kyle looked at properties. Though there were several desirable farms with renovated houses that should have been snapped up by Kyle, he didn't do so. He had the painful memory of Colleen begging him to buy a house. She wanted an old house they would have to renovate to make it uniquely their own. A house big enough for children…

He wrenched his thoughts away from those troubling waters. They returned to the village. A street sign caught his attention.

"Featherstone Lane," he read aloud. "What ideas that name evokes. Is it a dead-end street?"

"Yes. It's named for three generations of a family who used to live here. Come to think of it, their old house is for sale. But it must be run-down because it's been empty for a long time."

"Won't hurt to take a look at it," Kyle said, surprised at the stirring of an unexpected anticipation.

The house was a sorry sight. It would take a fortune to fix it. He had to be out of his mind to even consider it. Yet, its charm drew him. He could visualize it restored.

Colleen would have loved it. He pushed aside the stab of guilt. Two years, too late, came his desire to buy a house like the one she had wanted.

"Can you set me up with the realtor, Gary?"

"You aren't serious? Look at it. It's ready to fall down. The inside must be even worse."

"I want to see it," Kyle insisted. He grinned. "It'll be a challenge and that's what I need to make me forget work and the past." He pulled out the FOR SALE sign and tossed it into the weeds. "The location, at a dead-end lane and with all those fields in back, appeals to me. Private and yet the rest of Hawthorne is a short walk away. The benefits of the country without its isolation."

He gave a laugh. "I'm not a real country person. I like being near a neighbor or two."

Gary slapped Kyle's back. "I know what you mean." He was silent and then asked, "Are you going to be content living here alone? It's a big place."

"Of course. I'm with people all day. It'll be good to be by myself."

Even as these words left his lips, Kyle knew he lied. True, it would be good to get away from business associates and employees. Well, most employees. Cassandra Brown would be an exception. He wanted once more to have a special woman in his life. To fall in love again. It was time.

"Come up to the house," Gary invited. "We can see the end of the game. It's too late to contact the realtor today."

After supper Cassie walked down Featherstone Lane to the house. She immediately saw that the FOR SALE sign had been thrown aside. Her first impulse was to pick it up and stick it upright.

She looked at the area where the sign had been. The beaten down weeds indicated several people had been there. She had a sinking feeling that the house had been sold.

Because of the gathering darkness she didn't go, as she often did, to the back of the house to look at the rolling fields filled with wild flowers.

Without warning her old fear of the man swept over her.

After the accident she had struggled with her amnesia. She realized now that she had remembered bits and pieces of it, but not all of it. One part that eluded her was the fear she had of a man who wanted to hurt her. She couldn't remember what he looked like or why he frightened her. As time went on and no one came to the village, she forgot the fear and the man.

Until tonight.

She began to walk as quickly as she could. She gave a gasp as a dark car stopped beside her.

"Cassie, can I give you a lift?" Gary asked. He looked closely into her ashen face. "What's the matter? Is someone bothering you?"

Cassie gave a shaky laugh. "I let my imagination get the best of me. Yes, I'd like a lift. I overdid my exercise."

"You should have the hip operation," Gary said.

"I'm giving it serious consideration."

"Good." At her door he informed her, "Kyle is here this weekend."

"He must find the village of Hawthorne quaint after living in a big city like Broderick," she said.

"He likes it here."

"That's good. Thank you for the lift. Have a good night."

She quickly unlocked her door and entered. Inside, she leaned against the door. Broderick. The name of this city three hundred miles to the west of Hawthorne triggered a new memory.

She had shopped in Macy's to buy—

Then the image vanished. Lately, she'd had other brief, frustrating flashbacks. Her doctor had told her this would happen so she wasn't going to get upset. Still...

She slid to the floor, her forehead resting on her knees. Was this a false memory because she wanted to be connected with Kyle? She didn't know. There was a familiarity about him as though she had known him. Had she applied for work in Broderick? She didn't remember doing so. Wouldn't he have said something if this was true?

The flashback to Broderick made her think of her auto accident. She hadn't done so for many months.

As far as she knew, she had recovered all her memory after the accident—except for the man who scared her. As was usual, she didn't remember the actual crash. The tractor trailer had crossed into her lane and hit her little old Volkswagen head-on. Volunteer firemen had pulled her out before the car burst into flames.

She suffered severe head and body injuries. Fortunately, the accident occurred near Hawthorne which had a modern hospital heavily endowed by the Chandler family.

Dr. Gary Madison, a famed plastic surgeon, lived in the village. He took on the case pro bono of the unknown female victim who recovered from temporary amnesia. Cassandra Brown was able to help him reconstruct her face—or so she thought at the time. Later, she had pushed aside any doubts about the authenticity because she was very satisfied with the "new" face. She knew her voice wasn't the same, but that didn't bother her. In fact, she liked it. It seemed to be pleasing to other people as well.

Though her purse and other belongings and identification burned in the car, she remembered her name early on. The other facts of her past came flooding back. Lately, she had the feeling that she hadn't remembered it all. Almost as though she recalled it, up to a point in time only.

Also she couldn't explain the fear she had about a man wanting to hurt her. There was nothing in her life to make her a danger to anyone. Yet, she'd have this feeling of being in danger.

Her computer skills were intact. She had a very good position in Chandler Corporation in Spencer and lived happily in Hawthorne.

A hip operation would correct her limp, but the painful time she spent while her face and other injuries were being taken care of remained. Then, too, she wanted to test a man's affection for her. She longed for Mr. Right to come into her life.

With Kyle's decision to relocate in Spencer, it felt as though Kyle and she were fated to meet. Why the word "again" wanted to get into the sentence, she didn't know. It was so strange. Kyle must remind her of a past friend, one she'd known prior to the accident. It was the only explanation she came up with.

Tomorrow was Memorial Day and a holiday. Would Kyle come for his trail ride? She had to stop thinking of him all the time. He probably didn't even know she existed as a woman. Still her thoughts filled with him. It wasn't all her imagination that he looked at her with interest shining in those dark brown eyes.

Tomorrow she'd see him.

Memorial Day celebration was a solemn affair held in the hilltop cemetery. American flags fluttered over the grass-covered plots of those who had served this country in many wars. An amazing number in all.

When the memorial service was over, Cassie walked slowly down the hill.

"That was very impressive," Kyle said to Cassie as he appeared at her side. A gasp of surprise escaped from her. She stumbled and grabbed his arm. A hot, tingly sensation raced through her. Her insides quivered. It had to be from the sudden shaft of sunshine that poured over her. It couldn't be because she clutched his muscular arm.

"Yes, it was," she agreed. "I remember how I felt last year. That was my first experience with how a small village honored their dead in such a moving way."

"Then you aren't a native of Hawthorne?"

"No."

"How long have you lived here?"

"Two years. I got such wonderful treatment at the hospital after my car accident I wanted to live here." She said no more, feeling shy and uncertain.

Kyle's gaze fell to her right leg. "Is that how you hurt your hip?"

"Yes." Cassie added quickly, "Gary Madison was there that night, and he saved my life. I'll never forget what I owe to his medical skill."

Though she felt Kyle had more questions, he didn't ask them.

"I'm sorry if I've made you think about a painful time in your life."

"I've put it behind me. I try to be objective about the whole thing."

Though Cassie felt Kyle didn't believe her, she was glad he didn't continue the subject.

"May I take you to lunch?" he asked.

Lunch at the Sugar Shack had been pleasant. The conversation didn't touch on personal topics. Kyle watched Cassie relax and enjoy herself. He wouldn't refer to her accident. He wondered why he wanted to protect this woman, to make her happy. To see the dimple in her cheek work when she smiled and laughed. He recalled how he had always kissed Colleen's again and again.

Ah, that was another time, with another woman.

Cassie pushed her plate aside.

"Finished?" Kyle asked.

"Yes, thank you. I enjoyed sharing today's observances with you."

Belatedly, Cassie remembered he was her employer. When she saw him in Hawthorne, she forgot this fact. It was as though he shed that role and assumed another one.

At work, he made no attempt to see or to talk to her. She got glimpses of him walking briskly down the hall or disappearing into another office door. It always made her smile and her heart leap. The day was brighter. Such a silly, romantic response, but, nevertheless, it happened. After two long years she felt alive and happy.

They left the restaurant. Kyle guided her down the street and around the corner.

"Where are we going? I'd like to get back to my apartment."

Kyle kept up a slow pace, mindful of her limp.

"Is there a destination to this walk?" Cassie had to ask.

"Bear with me. I want to show you the house I just bought. I'm making Hawthorne my home."

"Hawthorne? What about Broderick?"

"My mother still lives in the family home. I will stay here. It's time for a new start."

"Oh," was all Cassie uttered. Joy filled her, and happiness strummed over the strings of her heart. She'd see Kyle often, not just at work.

"This is Featherstone Lane," Cassie exclaimed. Her pace quickened and her limp became more pronounced. When Kyle stopped in front of the last house, Cassie exclaimed, "You're the new owner!"

Chapter 2

"The closing was yesterday. What do you think of it? I know it's going to need a lot of fixing—"

"It's wonderful. I've always loved this house."

Kyle turned Cassie to face him, his hand on her arm. He saw the radiant glow in her eyes and the smile on her lips. Excitement seemed to stream through her skin to warm his hand. He wanted to draw her into his arms and kiss her. He caught himself at the last moment.

Happiness filled him at her approval. Would Colleen have reacted in the same way had he bought her a house when she asked? He knew, with deep regret, he had missed a priceless moment in their lives. More and more, he realized how much he had erred in his marriage. Never again. He was going to learn from his mistakes. Now he wanted to go forward and make a new life for himself with no regrets. At least, this house was the first step in that direction.

And it warmed his heart to watch Cassie's eyes shine with delight and to see how excited she was.

"May I depend on you to help me as I fix it up?" he asked.

Cassie laughed "Just try and—"

Cassie felt her face turn pink. She clapped her hand over her mouth. She had been about to tell Kyle her plans for the house. He would have ideas of his own. It would probably reflect the cold, formal interior of his family house.

A chill crept up Cassie's spine. How did she know about his family house in Broderick? She had never been there.

"How about it?" Kyle asked, interrupting her thoughts.

"If you want any suggestions, I'll be happy to give them," she answered finally.

"Do you want to go inside?"

Cassie saw his excitement. "Yes, let's go inside," she said quickly. His smile was her reward.

They picked their way up the grassy walk. Kyle helped her up the slanted steps to the front door.

Cassie could hardly contain her excitement. At last, she was going to do more than look in the windows.

Kyle pushed the door open. He held out his hand to her. She placed hers in his warm one, and her eyes looked into his. And she didn't see the board lying inside the threshold. She stumbled and started to fall forward. Strong hands caught her. The next thing she knew, Kyle picked her up and carried her into the house.

"Whoa," he said, laughing, "I didn't know we had an obstacle course here."

He set her down on a good section of the floor in the entrance hall.

Cassie's heart thudded in her chest. Her breath caught in her throat. Kyle had carried her across the threshold, just as a husband would carry his bride into their new home. When she looked at him, she breathed a sigh of relief. He hadn't had such a thought. His face was bland, and his smile innocent.

Cassie wished she could control her romantic fantasies of Kyle Chandler. If she had to have them, they should rightly be for Gary, the man who had saved her life. She should be in love with Gary in the time-honored tradition of a patient falling in love with her doctor. This hadn't happened, not for a moment.

"Let's start our tour with the living room," he said. Though there was no need for it, he took her hand in his. She loved the feel of his strong fingers and his tightening clasp.

Looking around, he shook his head. "This is worse than I first thought."

The floor was warped, the wallpaper stained and parts of the ceiling had fallen down. Debris littered the room. Old cardboard covered several broken windows. The fireplace was crumbling.

He steeled himself to get Cassie's reaction.

Her gaze swept over the room. She walked slowly to the double window that overlooked the fields at the back of the house.

"What a gorgeous view! You'll see fabulous sunsets from this room." She turned and looked around. "Really, Kyle, most of what has to be done here is easily repaired. Some sheet rock and wallpaper. The wooden floors can be sanded and polished. Thick throw rugs scattered around—"

Cassie stopped and saw Kyle smiling at her, his gaze warm and encouraging. It reached into her soul.

"Go on," he urged. "I was ready to throw the towel in. I didn't make a mistake buying a house that needs work."

"That's the fun and the challenge," Cassie said. "You can do it. Just take your time."

Cassie wandered into the dining room. She visualized a restored room. Flocked green wallpaper, an oriental rug covering the floor, an oval table for eight—big enough for a family Thanksgiving dinner. Sheer white curtains with a deep border of embroidered lace. No heavy drapes but a deep scalloped cornice on top of the windows.

Remembering she wasn't going to be the hostess here, her enthusiasm slipped away. This wasn't her house. Kyle was the owner. He would fix it up to please the woman important in his life.

Rebellion filled Cassie. Life wasn't fair. She hated to accept the reality of it. She wanted to be that woman. The glow left her eyes. She turned a sober face to Kyle.

"What's wrong? A minute ago you were glowing with excitement."

He put his finger under Cassie's chin. He looked deep into the blue eyes that suddenly were familiar, as though he had gazed into such a pair of Irish blue eyes many times in the past. For a second, the floor beneath his feet seemed to move, and Kyle wondered what was happening to him. When a hesitant smile curved Cassie's lips, a remembered dimple flashed briefly. He bent his head, wanting to kiss the dimple as he always did—

Kyle dropped his hand and stepped back, out of harm's way. Whatever had he been thinking? This woman wasn't Colleen; she was Cassandra Brown. Colleen's eyes and dimple were lost to him. It was certain he hadn't found them in Cassie. Still, it was an unnerving experience.

He saw Cassie take a deep breath. She backed away from him. "I need to go now," she said.

Before Kyle could reply, she limped out of the room, down the hall and out the door.

"Wait," he called but Cassie had already reached the street without a backward glance. She was running away from him. She had seen his desire to kiss her and wanted none of it.

His fist hit the wall. Surely, he hadn't frightened her. But her distress was out of proportion to a possible kiss. He wondered what past experience with men had caused Cassie to act this way. He again felt a great need to protect her. He had known her only a few weeks. Perhaps it was the limp that triggered the initial feeling. Or was it the haunting shadow in her beautiful blue eyes?

When was the car accident? He'd ask Gary. Once he had more information, he could be more objective about her. At least, Cassie had been happy he bought the house. She saw the possibilities and wasn't concerned with the drawbacks.

Drawbacks there certainly were. He'd have to get contractors in as soon as possible. He wondered how long it would take. He had never been concerned about a house and its upkeep. His mother managed everything with seemingly little effort. She always refused Colleen's offer to help.

Kyle locked the door. As he walked to his parked car he thought about his mother and her relationship with Colleen. Since he had been madly in love with his beautiful wife, he had automatically assumed everyone, including his mother, adored her, too. He knew now he had paid little attention to Colleen's attempts to discuss the home situation.

"We need to talk," Colleen begged at breakfast that fateful day in April. "I need you."

"Not now, darling," he said. Under the hall light, Colleen's skin was pale and her dress hung limply from her shoulders.

"Your mother—"

"Please, not that again! Work it out between you." The irritation in his voice made Colleen shrink away from him. Feeling guilty, he pulled her into his arms and kissed her.

"Sorry, forgive me, but I do have to run."

Kyle looked back at Colleen and saw the tears in her eyes. For a second he was tempted to go back to her, but his cell phone rang and the moment was lost.

That was the last time he saw Colleen.

The despair in her eyes still haunted him. If only he had gone back and straightened out the problems. If only, he had worked less and paid more attention to his wife whom he truly loved and adored. If only, he'd been a good husband, but he hadn't been. Yet, it was her decision to leave him; he hadn't left her. But, what was lacking in him? His self-confidence received a blow. He hadn't fulfilled all her needs or she would never have left him.

He would never forget his mother's call later that day at the office.

"Kyle, dear, Colleen has left you."

Colleen had scrawled a note of explanation and placed it on the hall table.

Kyle, darling, I've tried, truly I have tried, but I can't take it anymore. Besides, things keep happening that make me afraid but I can't explain. Give me some time. Don't come after me.

Love, Colleen

He had been bewildered and deeply hurt. And filled with guilt because he hadn't taken time to listen to her pleas that morning. Afraid? Of what, for heaven's sake? It made no sense. So she didn't want him to follow her—where? He'd have to wait to hear from her.

After an anxious week of not hearing from her, he took matters into his own hands. He hired a private investigator who wasn't pleased to follow a cold trail.

Colleen had taken only a small overnight case. Because she often took her rings off to apply lotion to her hands, her rings were on her dresser. She hadn't taken any other jewelry. Neither could she take her car for it was in the garage for repairs. Nor boarded a plane. It was impossible to get any information about train or bus travel. As time went on, neither did she use her credit cards or cash a check.

Kyle told the investigator, "Colleen always carried large amounts of cash no matter how much I objected. She could be very stubborn about things."

Thankfully there were no accounts in the papers or on the news about any crimes or accidents involving a woman of Colleen's description. She seemed to have disappeared. He also knew that his wife was brilliant, capable of planning a perfect disappearance if she wished. Since she also was a topnotch technical computer writer and programmer, she would be able to find work easily to fulfill her financial needs.

It wasn't like her to stay away without calling him. She loved him, he knew, and found it impossible to accept her actions. Yet, as weeks became months, and still no word, he came to believe that Colleen wasn't coming back to him. Maybe she didn't love him as much as he had thought.

His mother urged him to get on with his life.

"You must forget Colleen. She didn't really love you or she wouldn't have left you. So utterly heartless—not a word and no closure. You mustn't waste a thought on her. She doesn't deserve your consideration."

A year and a half later he finally gave in to his mother's advice.

Colleen hadn't responded to the legal notices he'd advertised around the country. Sadly, he divorced her on the grounds of desertion.

His mother objected to his decision to move to Spencer, but he had to start the healing process in his own way.

Buying the house in Hawthorne was also the right move. A new life—and, maybe, a new woman to love.

Chapter 3

From the doorway of the Chandler cafeteria, Kyle watched Cassie. She sat at a table by the window with a group of women. She stopped laughing long enough to pop the last piece of a brownie into her mouth and lick her fingers.

A warm feeling filled him. He knew he was infatuated with her. He wasn't ready to call it love. He had been with her only a few times. Besides, he kept remembering Colleen and the way she left him. He could never fully trust another woman.

It hadn't been love at first sight with Colleen either. It had been love at first kiss—under the mistletoe at the office Christmas party in Broderick.

Kyle left the cafeteria and returned to his office. He stood in front of the window. The work needing his attention lay on his desk. He resented his lack of concentration. He even resented Cassie. She had no right to disrupt his life.

What was her attraction? It wasn't only her beautiful face. True, there was something about the blue eyes and the dimple—

He shook his head. It was wrong to see Colleen's features in another woman. It wasn't fair to Cassie.

Kyle gave a rueful laugh. He was in one heck of an emotional mess. Two women, not one, were bothering him. Until he could keep them separate, he should do nothing—if he could.

He attempted to see or speak to Cassie every day at work. Depression set in if it didn't happen. He was acting like a teenage boy with a terrific crush on the head cheerleader.

Standing out of sight by his window, he watched her get on her bus. Each day he wanted to run down three flights of stairs to stop her. To take her to his car and drive her to Hawthorne.

All these things and more, he had been thinking ever since he carried Cassie over the threshold of his house. She hadn't noticed the significance of his action, but he hadn't been able to forget it. A beloved wife was carried into her husband's house...

How right she had felt in his arms. So slight in weight. She could do with a few more pounds to round out her charms.

Colleen...

There, he did it again. He had been about to say Colleen needed to regain the weight she had lost before she left him.

Colleen.

Would he ever stop thinking about her? He still dreaded reading in the newspaper the account of a car accident or plane crash. To see the report of her death. In some way, that sad fact would be better than the limbo he was lost in.

Why hadn't she called him or answered the legal notices in the papers? It was hard to believe that she had cut him out of her life in such a cruel manner. Of course, she could be very stubborn and set in her way. He'd had a hard time getting her to marry him. He remembered her arguing against marrying her boss—and moving in with his mother in the family mansion.

She had evidently made up her mind to leave him on her own. She hated to argue and would often maintain a stubborn silence. She had made a clean break, taking nothing from him. Yes, she was an independent, self-reliant person. She could take care of herself as she had done all her life. But, still, she wasn't cruel or thoughtless. And he was sure she loved him. Yes, there was a mystery here. Someday he hoped it would be solved.

Kyle shrugged his shoulders and went to his desk. He put aside his troubling thoughts and got to work.

After glancing over her shoulder Cassie saw Kyle leave. When he saw her lick her fingers, she felt her cheeks get hot. She had a feeling he watched her from his window as she got on the bus each day. She had even stumbled yesterday because she was thinking too much about him and not on the difficulty of getting up the high step of the bus.

Whenever she saw him, her heart would sing. She felt as though she were floating above the treetops into the heavens above. And, sometimes, it seemed he was there with her.

It had been so long since she had this joyous, giddy feeling...

Strange how fate worked. She remembered how breathless she had become at the first sight of him. An awareness she immediately buried. He wasn't in her league. All he could be was her employer. But her dreams continued.

Though he promised himself not to think about Cassie, at five o'clock Kyle was at the window, watching the bus pull in.

There she was. He frowned. Today she seemed to be walking slower, her foot dragging more than usual. Some days he noticed she would look up at his window. She didn't today, and he missed it. He knew he was being foolish, but he couldn't stop his heart from beating faster or having a grin curve his lips. She made him feel happy. It had been a long two years of depression and unhappiness. Yet, just by Cassie being there, his feelings took wing.

The bus pulled away.

He made an immediate decision to go to Hawthorne as soon as he finished his report.

An hour later, on his way out of town, he phoned the Nelson Bed and Breakfast and arranged to stay there for the weekend. After Gary and he had their ride, he'd have some of Cassie's cookies. He smiled as he wondered what kind they would be.

After he dropped off his suitcase at the Nelsons', he walked to his house. The lawn in front of the house needed to be seeded and the shrubs pruned. He'd get the local nursery to plant some flowers.

The outside of the house would be painted next week, white with Wedgwood blue shutters. Come to think of it, it was Cassie's suggestion.

Dusk descended. Kyle didn't want to enter an empty, dark house. Yearning filled him. Since Colleen left him, he had been alone. He wanted no more of it.

He started to walk back to the Nelsons'. Lost in his thoughts, Kyle almost bumped into Agatha and Emily Dixon, Cassie's landladies.

"Sorry, ladies," he said.

"No need to apologize," Agatha said. Of the two sisters, she did most of the talking. "You've been to your house. We're happy you're going to restore it. The Featherstone family lived there for over a hundred years. It was sad the family died out."

"What happened? I've been meaning to check out the previous owners."

Kyle offered an arm to each of the women. They walked along the wide sidewalk toward their house three blocks away.

"All three sons were killed in action in World War II. A very great tragedy. None of the boys had married. When the mother and father died after the war, it was the end of the family." Agatha gave a soft sigh. "Cassie always talked about how much she wanted the house and longed to buy it. Of course, since she has no money except her salary, she never could."

"Cassie never told me," Kyle said quietly.

"Oh, dear, perhaps I've said too much," Agatha murmured. "Cassie, however, never made a secret of how much she loved the house."

Agatha gave Kyle an arched look. "You should ask her to help you. That is, if your fiancée—"

"No fiancée—only an ex-wife."

Emily was the sister who said, "Good."

Kyle gave a hoot of laughter. So much said in one word, so much approval of his single status.

With still a block to walk before reaching the house, Agatha volunteered, "Cassie is good company for us. We love her dearly. Such a brave young lady. She endured so much pain for six months after the accident."

"What happened?"

"Outside of Hawthorne a tractor trailer crossed the line and hit her. Terrible, terrible injuries, everywhere. She also had amnesia but has recovered most of her memory." Agatha stopped walking. "She does get a few things mixed up so you have to excuse her."

Kyle nodded. "Can her limp be corrected?"

"Yes, but she doesn't want to go through another operation just yet."

"What about her face?"

"Thank goodness for Dr. Madison. Extensive plastic surgery made her as beautiful as she had been before the accident. When she recovered from her temporary amnesia, she was able to guide him. No one else knew what she looked like."

"When was this accident?"

"Let me think. Cassie has lived with us since last May, after her surgery. So the accident was on a rainy April night a year before. Two years ago, April fifteen, is the date."

April fifteen, two years ago, was the last time he had seen Colleen. Cassie had had her accident the same time.

Colleen.

Cassie.

Two tragedies, though unconnected, troubled him.

When the walk was over, he felt relieved.

"Would you like to come in for a cup of coffee?" Emily asked.

"Not tonight. It's been a hard week, and I'm going to bed early. I have an early trail ride with Gary tomorrow morning."

"Good night," Agatha said.

"Pleasant dreams," Emily said with a sweet smile. At the Nelsons', Kyle paced back and forth in his bedroom.

Two years ago, Colleen, the love of his life, had left without a trace.

Two years ago, Cassie Brown had been badly injured in a car accident—one that left her with a limp, a beautiful face and a husky voice he liked to hear.

Could Colleen also have suffered a blow or been in an accident and have amnesia? Was that why she never came back? She had said she needed time. He had taken heart that it meant she'd come back. But her picture had been shown around. Usually, an amnesia case got publicity. There had been none. No, Colleen changed herself and her way of life. She decided not to come back to him. Since she had no family, he couldn't get any help in that area.

He should have seen their marriage was in trouble. He recalled the weeks before she left. She stayed in her room most of the time. He shrugged it off as a fit of pique, at himself and his mother. Had there been fear in her eyes sometimes? But she had nothing to fear. No one would harm her. If only he had paid attention to all the signs.

What with being CEO of Chandler Corporation and helping his best friend, John Forest, start his campaign for governor, he had had no time for Colleen. Strange, he recalled Colleen had never liked John, had tried to get him to stay out of the grass roots campaign.

All these memories and learning Cassie's accident occurred during the same month and year as Colleen's disappearance made Kyle's dreams unsettled that night.

Friday afternoon the bus swung on time into its spot in front of Reilly's Drug Store in Hawthorne. Cassie saw Kyle's classic Camaro parked across the street.

I've always loved that car.

The memory flashed in and out of Cassie's thoughts.

She frowned. What was it she had just recalled? Something about Kyle's car. But how could she recall anything about his car? Oh, well, she had no interest in cars, at least none since the accident.

Later that evening, Cassie went about the task of making her cookies for Saturday. Her thoughts went back to her accident, triggered by the reason for making the cookies.

As was usual, she didn't remember the actual impact. She had been driving a secondhand Volkswagen. Her suitcase and purse, with all her papers and cash, burned in the fire. The stable hands were also volunteer firemen who had helped to rescue her and put out the fire. The burned-out shell of the car was in a junkyard.

She recalled being uneasy at seeing her new face. She played a game with herself. If this wasn't her true face then had she had a turned up nose? Or one that was large and had a hump in the middle because a classmate had whacked her with a baseball bat by mistake? Had freckles, big and brown, covered her cheeks? One or all of these, but certainly, never this almost Hollywood-perfect face she now had. Perhaps this was a face she longed to have when she was a dissatisfied teenager.

She told no one of her doubts. She felt relief that she had no family to be surprised or even dismayed at the possible changes. And the man she feared wouldn't know her either. That was a good thing, wasn't it?

She, however, had the distinction of having an original dimple since that cheek hadn't suffered any damage.

Sadness engulfed her. She was really alone in the world. Though the death of her parents and sister was long ago, tonight it felt like yesterday. But everyone in Hawthorne was good to her. The Dixon sisters were like dear aunts, the stable hands, her brothers. Gary wanted to be much more, but she couldn't feel for him any romantic emotion.

Kyle—oh, Kyle. He stirred the deepest depths of her soul. For some unknown reason, a feeling of kinship was very real, as though she had known him always. It was foolishness because they had known each other only a short time.

Perhaps there was something to the theory of reincarnation, that she had known him in many of her past lives.

Only last week the subject was tossed around at the lunch table.

"I personally believe in it," Liza said, "I was Queen Elizabeth!"
A burst of laughter rang out.

"I was Joan of Arc!"

"Me, I was with Columbus—the first woman to discover America!"
They had had a good time but were agreed that Cassie's was the best.

"I was with my Prince Charming again and again."

Whether the theory was true or not, she sensed a connection between Kyle and herself. A very personal, almost an intimate one. She had to keep reminding herself it wasn't so.

She hated being in limbo in a relationship with Kyle. She wanted Kyle to kiss her, to marry her, to take her into her dream house and make it theirs.

Cassie sniffed the air.

Heavens, while she was thinking deep thoughts, she was letting her cookies burn!

She flew to the stove and rescued the lot. A few, at the edge of the pan, were burned, but the rest were okay. She hoped the Dixon sisters didn't think she had set the apartment on fire. They might be elderly but their senses were still acute. She didn't want to upset them. She expected the aroma of the peanut butter cookies would drift to their part of the house, and they'd be down shortly for their sample.

Right on cue, a light tap came on the door.

"Come in," Cassie called.

Cassie's heart beat faster as she approached the riding stable. It was three o'clock. The stable hands were waiting for their weekly treat. A quick glance showed Kyle wasn't there. She didn't know whether to be glad or disappointed. Her feelings about him were in a constant turmoil.

"Peanut butter cookies, today," Cassie announced. "I made an extra batch, so there's plenty for everyone."

"You're the greatest," Smitty said and popped a whole cookie into his mouth. "Ummm," was his verdict.

Cassie took a cookie and imitated him. "Ummm."

"Must be awful good if the baker eats them," Kyle said. He stood close to her.

For a moment, Cassie couldn't move. Kyle's warm breath fanned her cheek. She took a slow, deep, breath and stilled the trembling of her hands. She turned to face him.

"Everyone gets some cookies," she said. "'Dems the rule,' as we used to say in school."

Kyle laughed and said to the group, "Come on, now, everyone?"

"Ummmm" filled the air.

Minutes later, Kyle said to her, "Let me carry the empty containers for you. Sure didn't take long to have every crumb disappear."

She smiled up at him. "It's worth every minute of effort on my part to bake these cookies." She looked away. "How's your house coming along?"

"Slower than I'd like. Most of the sheet rock has been installed."

She pursed her lips to keep blurting out her interest in every phase of the remodeling. She was silent on the drive back to her apartment.

"Would you like to come in for a cup of coffee?" she offered.

"I'm having dinner with the Nelsons. Another time."

"Sure. Have a good weekend."

Cassie forced herself not to look back and entered her apartment. Her hip ached. She suddenly felt depressed. She couldn't understand why her life wasn't as perfect as it had been before—before Kyle bought his house and was spending every weekend in Hawthorne. He was the disrupting force turning her world upside down.

She had been content before with her new life.

Since Kyle arrived on the scene, flashes from the past were more frequent. They disturbed and mystified her and made her feel insecure. How did she know she liked his car? Had she come from the Broderick area and perhaps seen it there?

If so, did the man she feared come from there? His face stayed just out of her memory's reach. It was frustrating not to remember and be held a hostage to fear.

What she needed was a session with Dr. Andrews, her psychotherapist. She reached for the phone.

Chapter 4

Cassie sat in the armchair across from Dr. Andrews. With a sigh, she closed her eyes and leaned her head against the back. Seeing a psychotherapist was on the advice of Dr. Madison. After the trauma of the accident and having plastic surgery on her face, it proved helpful. For the last year she had come for check-ups only. Today, questions brought her.

Dr. Andrews waited for Cassie to speak. She activated the tape recorder.

"I'm terrified at times," Cassie blurted out.

"Why is that?"

"Since my surgery, I've made a happy life for myself. Yet, I feel afraid at odd times. I think it's about the man I told you about."

"What triggered your fear this time?"

"I don't know. Saturday night was a normal night. I watched sitcoms and read the paper featuring Governor Forest's battle over civil rights. Out of the blue, I felt afraid. I even checked outside my door. No one was there, and I quieted down my breathing. I gradually convinced myself that I was safe. What's going on?"

Dr. Andrews took her time. "You evidently haven't recovered from your amnesia. This fear shows you've blocked out a painful incident in your life. Therefore, you conveniently forgot him. Until now. Has someone new come into your work force?"

"No. Same people. Same job."

"Someone moved into Hawthorne recently?"

Cassie started to say no and then stopped.

"Kyle Chandler, my boss, has bought a house in Hawthorne, but he doesn't make me feel afraid."

Cassie saw no need to confess what other emotions he aroused in her.

"What do you know about him?"

"He came from Broderick and has a condo in Spencer. He renewed his friendship with Dr. Madison. He's been going on trail rides with him. He's decided to buy a house and live in Hawthorne."

"Have you ever been in Broderick? Know any friends of Kyle Chandler?"

"Not that I remember."

Cassie closed her eyes. She didn't know anything about Kyle's past life there. But she did have flashes about Kyle's car and the inside of his mother's house. And feelings that were difficult to explain—as though she knew him or had known him intimately.

"Cassie, talk to me."

"You may be right about my blocking out a memory. Perhaps Kyle's coming into my life is stirring the pot. Maybe his physical appearance reminds me of another man in my life or even of the man I fear. Kyle knows about the accident, my amnesia and the plastic surgery. It's been two years, and he only came a short time ago to this area. If he had known me, he'd have said so by now."

Cassie realized her words were to reassure herself, not to give information to Dr. Andrews.

"So, what do I do?"

"Don't force it. If possible, let life go on as it has. If you have a panic attack, try to remember what happened before it—whom you were talking to, where you were or what you were looking at."

Cassie hesitated before asking the next question. "Do you think this man I'm afraid of is still out there and could actually hurt me?"

"I don't know. Until something definite happens, be careful. Protect yourself as much as possible but don't become paranoid. Call me if you need someone to talk to."

When she stepped out of the bus in Hawthorne, a chill ran down Cassie's spine. Because of her session with Dr. Andrews she had taken the last bus. The shadows cast by the trees were dark on the sidewalk. No one else walked the street in front of her. She chided herself for feeling afraid. This was Hawthorne, always dear and always safe. No killer lurked in the darkness. At least, she hoped not.

She took a deep breath. She wasn't going to be controlled by a runaway imagination.

She hadn't seen Kyle during the first days of the week. It was amazing how they could either miss each other completely, or find each other at every turn. This week, it was the former. She missed seeing him and knew she was being unrealistic. He was her boss. That he had purchased a house in her village didn't mean they would become close friends or whatever.

But Kyle acted like a friend. So much so, she forgot he was the CEO of the company.

But, on Friday morning, Cassie looked forward to her coffee break. On her way, she met Kyle holding a stack of folders—the ones from her department.

He smiled, the smile that made her heart beat faster.

"Do you have an appointment with Dr. Andrews after work?" he asked.

"No."

"Good," Kyle said. "Since I have to see the plumber at the house, I'll drive you home. Take the elevator to the parking garage, Level A. Wait for me at the elevator. Five o'clock. Don't be late."

He thrust the folders into Cassie's hands, gave another smile and was gone.

Before Cassie could utter a word.

The king had spoken, and she had to obey. This was a side of Kyle she didn't think about. She shouldn't be surprised he expected to have his orders obeyed without question. When had he gotten the idea she wanted to ride with him rather than go on the bus? Since she had no way to change his plans, she would meet him. But she didn't like his dictatorial attitude.

After gulping her coffee, Cassie hurried to complete the project she had been working on. She seethed with resentment at Kyle's manner. It had been a long time since a man had ordered her around. This much came back from the past, a past she had forgotten. She began to wonder how much more she hadn't remembered. She thought she recovered all of her memory.

No way.

There was a man she was afraid of. Was there a lover or even a husband? It was most disturbing. She realized that in the past year she deliberately chose to be content to drift from day to day in the happy glow of life in a small, safe village.

With the five o'clock meeting with Kyle constantly on her mind, Cassie did her work with greater speed than ever. She liked her work. She was also proud she had been promoted from senior tech writer to project manager. But she was often haunted by visions of future years of a stress-driven career. Surely she would find the man of her dreams, marry and have her own home. She tried not to put Kyle in her dreams.

Five minutes to five, Cassie leaned against the wall next to the elevator. She shifted her body to take the weight off her hip. When she got out of the hospital a year ago, she had used a walker. Then a cane. The look of pity in people's eyes made her cringe. Though the hip hurt more, she discarded the cane and trained herself to minimize the limp. More and more she thought of having the operation.

She also hated that Kyle saw a flawed woman.

He thoughtfully went out of his way to adjust to her dragging walk, to put his hand under her elbow—never mind the thrill his touch gave her.

Cassie closed her eyes and leaned against the wall.

"Tired?" Her eyes popped open. She hadn't heard the elevator stop.

"You didn't come down the elevator," she said.

Kyle gave a laugh. "I ran down the stairs fearing you wouldn't wait for me if I were a few minutes late."

"I wouldn't do that!"

"I wasn't going to risk it," he said, smiling down at her, teasing her.

"This way," he said, his hand under her elbow. A few minutes later, Cassie sank onto the soft leather of the bucket seat. It felt wonderful. She wouldn't think of the difficulty of getting out of it until they reached Hawthorne.

Kyle talked about the house.

"The construction is taking time, but I want this house to be perfect."

"Of course. Each change makes it more comfortable and, well, livable." Cassie took a deep breath. "I especially love the big deck in the back. You'll be able to watch the beautiful sunsets. The back fields of your property slope to the woods to give you a wonderful view."

"You really like my house."

Cassie smiled at him. "I saw its potential long before you did," she confessed. "If I had had the money I would have bought it the day after I discovered it. Of course, my renovations would have been minimal, not like yours."

"You don't resent—"

"Of course not. I'm happy you bought it before someone decided to tear it down." She gave a laugh. "I've been praying for just that."

"Only in relation to the house?" Kyle's question made Cassie's heart beat faster. She felt flustered and off base. She didn't dare read into the question more than he might be hinting.

"It was my only prayer. It's great to have it answered," she finally said.

Kyle gave a laugh and asked no more questions.

The car purred to a stop in front of her apartment. Cassie slipped off the seat belt and took a deep breath. She willed herself to endure, without cringing, the pain of getting out of the car.

The door opened.

Before she could swing her legs out, Kyle reached in. His arms slid under her, and he lifted her out of the car without effort.

Cassie gave a gasp of surprise. She had a moment to enjoy being in his strong arms, held close to his body.

He took his time putting her down, to her delight.

"Thank you. That was wonderful," Cassie said shyly. "I dreaded getting out of that bucket seat." She took a deep breath. "That settles it. In September I'll have my hip operation."

"Why wait until then?"

"I want to enjoy the summer and not spend it in the hospital. September is just around the corner."

Kyle saw her point, but he wanted her free from pain immediately. At least today, he had saved her from a few minutes of it. He recalled the times he watched her get on the bus. He hadn't thought that getting off the bus might be even more painful. Finally, she had made the decision to have the operation. In the meantime, he'd help her enjoy the summer.

Chapter 5

Later that evening Cassie sank into the hot bubble bath and uttered a sigh of pleasure. When she arrived at work, she had slipped on a stone on the sidewalk in front of the Chandler Building. She twisted her hip painfully. It ached all day. If she'd had her cane, it wouldn't have happened. Ah, vanity, vanity, thy name is woman! Wanting to enjoy her summer was only one reason for a September date for her operation. The other reason was economical. By then, she would have accumulated enough sick days. Her medical insurance would pay for the operation. She was so fortunate to be working for Kyle's company with their excellent insurance program.

She also didn't want Kyle to think of her as a cripple. Some men didn't want a relationship with an imperfect woman. And it would be wonderful to be normal again. Though, if a man truly loved a woman, a physical handicap shouldn't matter.

Love.

Kyle didn't love her, for heaven's sake. But, oh, when he touched her, her heart went crazy, and she could feel the heat on her cheeks. Had his light touch felt as though it had happened before? There was a mystical swirl of feeling around them at times, a sensation she couldn't explain.

As the bubbles in the tub circled her, she savored the memory of Kyle's arms when he lifted her out of the car. That day, when she stumbled on the threshold of his house, he held her for only a moment. Today, he hugged her close to him. He made her feel precious and fragile. Could he possibly want to take care of her?

As though he had done this before…

Cassie gave herself a shake, making the water slip over the rim of the tub and onto the floor. How foolish of her. Yet, the idea of a past with Kyle excited her. Had they been friends? Schoolmates? Even lovers?

Better not think about it. For, if she had known Kyle before, then the man she feared came from Broderick. Better not regain all her memory. Better live in her fantasy world in Hawthorne as long as possible. Whatever she knew that was dangerous to the killer still eluded her. Her mind, thankfully, was determined to protect her.

"I love you, Daisy," Cassie whispered into the ear of an Appaloosa mare the next afternoon. The mare nickered and pawed the ground of her stall.

"Do you ride?" Kyle asked, appearing suddenly at Cassie's side.

Cassie continued to stroke the mare. "Not now."

Her heartbeat quickened. Memory from the past surfaced without warning. She had ridden well and often on an Appaloosa.

"Is this horse your favorite?"

"Yes." Cassie gave Daisy another sugar treat. Suddenly, she remembered something else. "When I was a little girl I saw an old video *The Horse with the Flying Tail.* It was about an Appaloosa winning the Olympics. Ever since, that kind of horse was the only one for me."

The breath left Kyle's lungs, and his heart thundered. His wife

Colleen had had the same experience. What were the odds this could happen twice? Kyle looked intently at Cassie. She wasn't Colleen. It was just one of those million-in-one chances.

"What's wrong?" Cassie asked. "Why should my story upset you?"

"It's nothing. I recall someone I once knew talking about that old film. It just surprised me."

Cassie gave him a long stare, as though she weighed the truth of his answer. When she turned to leave, Daisy gave her a nudge. Low, happy laughter reached Kyle.

He whipped around at the sound of it—Colleen's lilt of laughter! It had always delighted him—but it was Cassie who had laughed and was now talking to the horse. He must be hallucinating. He shook his head to clear it.

"Here's your sugar. I'm sorry I forgot your last treat," Cassie said to Daisy.

Walking out of the stable, Cassie picked up her empty cookie tray from the top rail of the stall. It had been oatmeal raisin cookies today.

Kyle snatched at the last broken piece and grinned as he chewed on it.

"What kind will it be next week?"

"I don't know yet. Do you have a preference?"

"Please let it be chocolate chip. I'm sure no one will protest."

Cassie remembered those were the first of her cookies he had tasted. If nothing else, her cookies made an impression on him. Happiness sang in her at the thought.

Kyle fell into step beside her. His tall shadow moved along with him.

"Here's the latest on the house. The plumber's finished downstairs. Installing the hot tub upstairs will take time," Kyle reported. "The painters want to know what color. Will you help me?"

The rooms flashed before Cassie's eyes. Ah, yes, she knew the colors and wallpaper designs she wanted.

"What did you have at home?"

Kyle gave a crooked smile. "My mother liked white except in the main dining room. It had dark maroon flocked wallpaper that my great-grandfather had imported from France. He built the house, and each generation of the family has lived there. It's an elegant, traditional house."

"You want this house to be different, I assume."

"You assume right."

Cassie knew she should say "no." She was getting too involved. Slowly bits and pieces of her past life were surfacing. What would happen when she regained all her memory? It might not be the happiest day of her life. But she would be happy today, and do what she longed to do.

"Yes, I'll help you. You'll have to get the book with the paint colors."

"I already have it. Could we do it tomorrow, after lunch?"

When they reached her apartment, Cassie hesitated about asking Kyle to come in. So many thoughts and feelings were whirling inside her.

"Good night. I'll see you at your house tomorrow."

Turning to him, she looked into his dark eyes.

Kyle stood very close to her. If she swayed, she would touch him. She couldn't stop looking at him. She held her breath. Slowly his head lowered. He placed his warm lips on her inviting, up-turned mouth.

A tender, light kiss soon changed to one warmer and deeper. A moment later he stepped back with a soft laugh.

When he didn't kiss her again, keen disappointment filled her. She wanted Kyle to kiss her again and again. Then she realized they were standing in plain view of anyone passing by or looking out of a window. No wonder Kyle was smiling.

"Good night, dear Cassie. Thank you for helping me with my house."

His finger caressed her dimpled cheek, a touch felt deep within her. He took a deep breath, turned and walked away.

Cassie smiled, feeling as though she had suddenly gotten a ride on a cloud. For surely, her feet didn't touch the ground when she entered her apartment.

Kyle had kissed her.

He had truly laid his firm warm lips on hers. Whatever the kiss meant, it made her happy to be alive. For a long time she had been drifting, living a fantasy life.

He called her his "dear Cassie"—

Oh, if only she remembered all of her past, a past that held no potential of another man in it. She even wanted to know now about the man she feared so she could get rid of him. She needed to know about herself before she lost her heart to a man who might never belong to her.

Later, the ringing of the phone startled her.

"Cassie, it's Kyle. We can't meet tomorrow. I'm leaving immediately for Broderick because my mother has had a heart attack."

"I'm so sorry. I hope she feels better soon. I'll be thinking of you. Take care."

"I'll call you when I get back."

Cassie tugged at her hair. How quickly things changed. How important it was to seize each moment, to live life to the fullest and not waste a precious moment. She had no certainty that tomorrow would ever come; she only had today. Her thoughts would be with Kyle and his mother, for the best to occur in their lives.

A heart attack? His strong mother had had a heart attack?

Kyle's conscience flayed him. He hadn't gone back to Broderick for four weeks. Instead, Hawthorne had taken all his time and attention. Between working on his house and thinking of Cassie, he hadn't spent much time with his mother. That wasn't an excuse, even though her calls had been full of complaints. And his mother wouldn't give up talking about Colleen and her desertion.

He'd be sure to prevent misunderstandings between his mother and a new wife. When he decided to get one. He did love his mother and knew of her deep and boundless love for her only son. He'd learn from his past mistake. He would make certain his mother got to know Cassie. Not spring a stranger on her as he had done with Colleen. No wonder the two women had never bonded. When the time was right, things would be different.

But he wasn't ready to do this. Could he trust a woman? He had been certain that Colleen loved him—for the rest of her life, she had promised. Yet, she left him and broke his heart.

Trust, once broken, was not easily regained.

The engine of the corporate jet throbbed. Soon the private airfield in Broderick came into view. They glided to a smooth stop. He took a taxi to the hospital.

Kyle followed the nurse into his mother's room.

As soon as he entered the room, his mother's eyes opened. The hand she held out to him shook. To see his strong and vigorous mother so white and helpless shocked him.

"Mother," he said and grasped her hand. He leaned down to kiss her forehead. His mother always kissed him on the forehead or cheek—and then, rarely. Strange, he hadn't let this fact bother him before. No wonder he had welcomed Colleen's constant touches of affection, the hugs and the abundance of kisses.

"You've given me a scare," he said. "How long have you been hiding your condition from me?"

He saw his mother stiffened her spine. As he well knew, she hated to be questioned. Then, she relaxed and gave him a smile.

"Dear, this came as a complete surprise to me, too. Fortunately, it wasn't a full-blown attack. More like a warning."

"You'll beat it, Mother."

Later, when the nurse came to check on her patient, Kyle stood up. "You can see her the first thing in the morning," the nurse said. "I'll stay with her tonight."

Kyle kissed his mother again and laid his cheek against her head for a few seconds. Her hand gripped his. He didn't let his concern show. Instead, he whispered, "I love you, Mother."

He heard her gasp of surprise. He couldn't remember the last time he had voiced his love. He and his mother had never been openly affectionate or demonstrative. He was glad he had told her he loved her before he left her for the night.

45

At the family house, Kyle felt exhausted and depressed. His worry for his mother had drained him. He had thought she would always be there for him. He had also depended on the "forever after" aspect of his marriage to Colleen. She had left him as suddenly as his mother could have had her heart attack been fatal.

The fragility of life and the importance to seize this moment filled him.

Cassie.

No, he wasn't going to rush this relationship. His first and only kiss had marked him. He hadn't planned it and was surprised at the impact it had on him. The dazed look in Cassie's eyes had shown how it had affected her also. It had meant more than either of them had expected. It was important to move slowly from one phase to another in their relationship. He didn't want to make a mistake again.

The next day Kyle grasped his friend's hand. "Good of you to come, John," he said.

"Sorry to hear about your mother. How is she?"

"Doing as well as can be expected. Mother'll have to cut down on her social activities for a while."

"She'll be missed," John said.

"How are things at the governor's mansion? I'm proud of you." Kyle gave him a slap on his shoulder.

They had been friends since childhood. They drifted apart after college. John became immersed in politics while Kyle tended his family business. Kyle shoved aside the memory of hearing some unsavory gossip about his friend. It had to be untrue.

He recalled Colleen had never liked John. She urged him to stay away from him. One of their last arguments had been about the man. No sense in worrying about it now. It was good of John to come to the hospital this morning.

"Sorry, but Mother isn't up to having visitors today."

"I understand. Incidentally, have you heard from Colleen?"

The question surprised Kyle.

He shook his head. "Not a word since April fifteenth, two years ago. In this age of technology she's disappeared without a trace. I always knew she was capable of carrying out any plan."

"I shouldn't ask, but just why did Colleen leave you? I thought you had a happy marriage."

"As I look back, it was mostly my fault. I neglected her, and my mother didn't help. She wouldn't accept Colleen as a daughter-in-law. Of course, I was madly in love with Colleen from the beginning. How I ever let neglect and misunderstanding come between us I'll never know."

"Did Colleen appeal for help or something?" John went to stand by the waiting room window.

"Strange you should ask. The morning of the day before she left, she called me. She seemed especially agitated. She wanted me to come home immediately as she had something serious to discuss with me. I put her off. Said I'd see her at dinner."

Kyle paced the floor.

"Unfortunately, a business problem came up, and I didn't get home until midnight. During the next day, Colleen left."

Kyle felt again the hurt and despair of those early days of Colleen's departure.

"Later, when she didn't contact me or answer any of our legal notices, I accepted that she didn't want to be married to me anymore. The divorce is final. So, it's all over, and I'm going on with my life."

"You've stopped all attempts to find her?"

"Yes. It's over."

"I probably shouldn't butt in, but I think you should keep on. You'll never have complete closure until you know for certain where Colleen is living, and that she knows about the divorce."

Kyle looked at his friend. "You're right." He added, "I've met another woman." Cassie's sweet smile haunted him. He wanted everything right in his life before he told another woman he loved her and wanted her to marry him.

"All the more reason to keep looking for Colleen. Let me know how it goes. You'll do that, won't you?"

"Of course, John. I'll let you know any development. But don't hold your breath."

"Again, I'm about to give you more advice. Go slow with this new relationship. You must find Colleen first."

Kyle's heart sank. John was right. He would call his investigator tomorrow morning and reactivate the search. It wouldn't be fair to Cassie not to. Besides, hadn't he felt an ambiguity when he was caught, by surprise, at seeing Cassie's dimple and heard her laughter—as though it was a fleeting glimpse of Colleen? Why, oh, why did Cassie have that dimple, that laugh? At least her voice was her own and not like that of the other woman in his life.

Although he didn't require a woman to be beautiful, how fortunate for him that both women to claim his heart were truly beautiful. The coloring was the same, but Cassie's features were different—the eyebrows, the nose and the square chin. Colleen had been a true Irish beauty. Cassie, on the other hand, was beautiful in her own unique way.

And, sadly for him, both beauties weren't his mother's choice for him. She had steered him toward Alicia Tenant, a blond, English-rose woman, very elegant and serene. And much too cold and reserved for him. True, she would be the perfect social hostess, an untiring worker at all social functions and fundraisers for numerous charities. But he didn't want her; he wanted a woman of his choice, a warm and loving woman.

He saw, today, how out of place Colleen had been in his mother's world, no matter how hard she tried. How critical his mother had been of her efforts. Why hadn't he seen it then? Colleen had been unhappy. He hadn't found any time to listen and be with her.

He had been impatient with her request they buy their own house. He could still hear his words.

"Don't be absurd. Of course, we'll continue to live here with Mother. This is the family home."

Colleen's sad eyes haunted him today. Now he had a house, and no longer lived in the family mansion. Too late, much too late, for Colleen. Cassie would never live in Broderick, no matter what his mother had to say. That is, if she would have him. Because of his mother's health, he'd have to be careful how he introduced Cassie to her. He had learned some valuable lessons from his first marriage.

"Mr. Chandler, you may come in to see your mother," the nurse called.

Dr. Johnson was in the room.

"Good to see you, Kyle. Your mother is doing fine. I'd like her to stay here for a week." He wiggled his finger at Mrs. Chandler's protest. "A week, to do all the tests. Also, mainly, to let her rest. Since you moved to Spencer, she's been doing too much."

Kyle nodded as guilt flooded him.

"Mother, I'll stay with you this week," Kyle promised.

"Thank you, son."

He wondered if Cassie would miss him. He would give her a call and let her know his plans.

Chapter 6

Cassie tried to picture what Kyle's mother looked like and failed. Kyle's remarks about the family mansion didn't quite fit her initial image of an easygoing, maternal figure. Maybe someday she would meet her. She could understand his need to stay with his mother. How fortunate that she was recovering and going home soon.

On Sunday afternoon Cassie went to Kyle's house. She admired the velvet lawn and the flowerbeds the local greenery had planted. It looked picture perfect. Yet, she would have planted different flowers. Made the beds less formal. More like an English cottage garden. She liked delphinium and columbine against the house. She looked again at the flowers. Where were her beloved hollyhocks? And geraniums and impatiens should be more in evidence. An old fashioned petunia should be there, too.

She walked slowly to the back of the house. She looked down the gentle slope of the fields. There was a long field between the house and the dense woods that marked the end of Kyle's property.

A dream of the future tantalized her imagination. A maze, an English maze! There was room for one. Of course, those in England had been planted hundreds of years ago and were of great height and depth. But wasn't it possible to use quick growing American shrubs and have a reasonable maze in a short time? What fun it would be!

Cassie threw up her arms and hands to the heavens and gave a happy laugh. As long as she was daydreaming, she might as well dream big! Yes, definitely, a maze in the back yard.

She also imagined a sweet and loving Mrs. Chandler who welcomed a daughter-in-law who wasn't in their social circle.

Slowly, reality reared its head. She sat on the top step of the deck. Hugging her knees, she laid her head on them. Tears slowly ran down her cheeks.

It was hard to be apart from Kyle. During the day she kept busy and didn't think of him constantly. It was a different story in the dark, quiet hours. When she crawled into bed, she felt like she was in a dark hole with no light in sight.

She thought longingly of the happy days and weeks before Kyle came into her life. She had been so content just coasting along, happy with her pleasant, quiet life in Hawthorne. But, even then, she knew those days were numbered. Change had to come. It came with the advent of Kyle in her life. Truly, she wouldn't have it in any other way.

On Friday morning, Kyle stepped on the accelerator of his car as he sped east toward Hawthorne. The last three weeks had been difficult. At last, his mother was home and obeying the doctor's orders.

Because he had an entire weekend to spend in Hawthorne, happiness filled him. After the trail ride Saturday morning with Gary, he would have some of Cassie's cookies. He felt like a little boy looking forward to a treat.

He'd be at the house Saturday afternoon. Again on Sunday. Could he persuade Cassie to be with him both times?

As the car climbed the village hill, Kyle saw the American flags decorating the poles. The flowers in the curbside tubs were red, white and blue.

July Fourth week. He had forgotten.

How festive the village looked. A wave of pride filled him. This was his home now, and it felt wonderful. He had never had this identification with the city of Broderick. He even questioned whether he truly called the family mansion home. With his mother mellowing since her near brush with death, perhaps there would be a change there, also.

He waved to Cassie's landladies, disappointed that Cassie wasn't with them. He pulled into the Nelson driveway. His room was always ready for him. It would be good to have a cup of coffee with the Nelsons. He could depend on them to give him the news and gossip since he was last here.

He'd hear about Cassie. She was a favorite with them. Mrs. Nelson's face was bland. "Cassie is beautiful."

Kyle grinned at her. "No argument from me. I look forward to her cookies tomorrow."

"Don't we all." She added, "Cassie has gone to visit friends in Spencer."

Well, he now knew where she was. That he wouldn't see her today. His world was suddenly empty and lonely.

"Ummm," was the consensus the next day. Soft, three inch in diameter and iced half in chocolate and half in white, the cookies disappeared like magic.

"Make more the next time," came the request.

Cassie's laughter filled the stable yard. Her dimple flashed, and her blue eyes sparkled. Kyle wasn't the only one who thought her bewitchingly beautiful.

Kyle wanted to pull her into his arms and hold her forever. To kiss the laughing lips and the illusive dimple as he had done many times before—

Shock, then dismay, pulsated through him. Cassie's laughter reminded him of Colleen's. He was seeing and hearing his ex-wife everywhere. Without a doubt, he couldn't start a serious relationship with Cassie until he located his first wife and made sure she had no place in his life.

John was right.

He had to have absolute closure.

But was it possible for him to erase from his memory and his heart the deep love he had had for Colleen? How did one do that? Sure, he thought about her less and less as time went by. But did true love ever die? He was in an emotional turmoil. Feelings for Cassie filled his heart. Could these wipe out or override his memories? Definitely, he had to end his old life before he could start a new one.

The inner argument went on. Others, however, had more than one love relationship and been happy in the second one. Perhaps, so could he. But how did they do it? Was there a book describing the process?

He turned to speak to Cassie.

She had left the stable and not waited to talk to him. Disappointment and resentment burned in him. He'd been gone for weeks. It meant nothing to her? He'd go to her and find out why. But first, he'd tie up the last loose ends and call his investigator.

Kyle pulled out his cell phone and made his call.

"Yes, I know the trail is cold. However, I want you to start over."

He listened to the reply.

"Cost is no problem. Put more men on the case."

The call completed, he went to Cassie's apartment. Cassie came around the corner of the house holding a bouquet of tulips and lilacs. She gave him a shy, radiant smile over the flowers. She made a breathtaking picture; one he'd never forget.

He had to have this woman, he thought.

She meant everything to him.

It was as though the love he had had for Colleen flowed to Cassie in a deep, intense way. He felt it wasn't a betrayal of his first love—only an extension of it. Or it seemed to him this was the best way to explain it.

Colleen took herself out of his life; he hadn't been unfaithful, nor had he ceased loving her at the time she left. He was aware of his failings as a husband. It was a blow to his feeling of self-worth and confidence. Would he be the same in another relationship? Could he ask another woman to trust him?

After time passed, he did what was necessary. However, no matter what the lawyers assured him, he'd like to make it final in his heart by having her sign the papers in his presence, to declare she no longer loved him in any way. To free him in order to fall in love again.

He stopped thinking of the past. In front of him was Cassie, his love now.

"Please come with me to the house," he asked. He held out his hand. Cassie grasped it. She looked steadily at him, happiness making her spirits soar. It was so good to have him back.

"Yes. Let me get a vase. We'll take these flowers to your house. You can enjoy them there."

Arriving at the house, they both admired the progress.

The kitchen had been enlarged. The oak cabinets gleamed, and the butcher-block counter blended in. Cassie slid her hand along the smooth surface. She looked at the far end of the room.

"I'm glad you had a fireplace built. How perfect it'll be to sit before it this winter."

Kyle smiled at her. It would be perfect if she were there with him.

"What do you think of the wraparound deck?" he asked. "I've left the old-fashioned porch in front. I wasn't sure this combination would work, but I'm pleased with it."

Cassie walked out of the kitchen to the deck. It faced the fields in back. The place where she had put her maze. It would be such fun to watch people in the maze—and rescue them if they couldn't find their way out.

"Why are you smiling?" Kyle asked. "That look says you have a secret."

Cassie shook her head. "Sorry, I can't tell you. Perhaps, sometime."

Kyle chuckled.

They walked back into the house. The downstairs powder room needed wallpaper.

"A print with blue flowers?" she asked.

"You decide," Kyle said. Since this would be Cassie's home, she should decorate it. He glanced down at her. How sweet she was. His heart filled with tenderness for her. A wave of happiness unfurled within.

It was good to be happy again. For the past two years he had felt only cold and emptiness. Work filled his days and nights. The family business thrived but at a great expense to his emotional life. Realizing this, he made the move to Spencer, a big change, even if only a geographical one, to start with.

While Cassie and Kyle picked the wallpaper, darkness fell. The overhead electric lights didn't make the empty rooms inviting.

"Enough for one day," Kyle decided and guided Cassie outside the front door. "How about some dinner? Sharon Springs Inn—"

"No, no, thank you," Cassie interrupted. "I have things to do tonight. Another time."

Kyle realized Cassie wanted to keep their relationship on a casual level. She'd help him with his house but no more.

"Tomorrow afternoon at two?" he asked. "We'll make some paint decisions."

Cassie hid her disappointment at his easy acceptance of her rejection. So it had only been a casual request.

"Come, I'll walk you back to your apartment."

"I'd like that."

Cassie was relieved to have Kyle carry on a conversation of this and that.

He left her at the door. His farewell was a casual, "See you around."

Cassie entered her apartment. She slid the curtain aside from the slim window next to the door. She watched Kyle walk away. She wanted desperately to change her mind, to call him back and go out to dinner with him. He was everything she wanted in a man. But he was her employer, and he was rich. And, somehow, came the feeling that his mother might be a big problem. Why did things have to be so complicated and impossible?

The next afternoon Kyle appeared early at Cassie's apartment.

"Hi, thought we'd walk together."

"That would be wonderful."

As they went down the walk, he glanced back at the house. Her landladies peered out their parlor window. They smiled, and he waved to them. He grinned.

The pink flush on Cassie's cheeks made her even more beautiful. She turned her head away from him. She started walking as fast as she could. He gave a low whistle, matching his steps to hers. Once they turned the corner, they were out of the Dixon's sight.

Kyle gave a low laugh. He reached over and took Cassie's hand. She looked at him. For a minute he thought she was going to pull away. When she didn't, he smiled at her. He clasped her hand a little tighter. The warmth from her palm engulfed his fingers.

To show such affection in the bright afternoon sun made a statement to anyone who saw them. And there were quite a few out walking on this beautiful summer day. Cassie's cheeks remained pink but she let her hand remain where it was. When they got to the house, Kyle didn't know whether her sigh was one of relief or regret. The latter was his hope.

Deciding on paint colors took an hour. Afterwards, they went outdoors and sat on the top step of the deck gazing at the beautiful panorama before them.

Suddenly, Cassie jumped to her feet and pointed her finger. "Look, there's a deer at the edge of the woods!"

"Guess I'll have an animal preserve on my land," he said. "No hunting allowed, don't you agree?"

"Oh, yes."

They watched until the deer disappeared.

"Just think," Kyle said, "I'll become a permanent resident of Hawthorne when the painters are finished."

"That'll make you happy.

"I made the right decision to set down roots here. I also like the work situation. Spencer is different from Broderick. The stress is much lower, and the employees seem happy in their jobs."

He hoped this was true for Cassie. Under her capable direction as project manager her department ran smoothly.

"Are you going to the parade tomorrow?" Cassie asked.

"I wouldn't miss it. I'm sure Broderick had one, but I never attended."

"You'll be impressed with this parade. For a small village, it does itself proud with all the bands and floats. It meant so much to me last year. In June I had the last surgery on my face. No more hospitals for me. The Fourth of July became my personal Independence Day."

"You don't have to answer," Kyle said, "but how did you feel just before the last bandage came off?"

"Scared and worried," she said. "Although Gary had all the pictures, I still was afraid there would be scarring and I'd look terrible."

When Kyle gently took her into his arms, Cassie's past thoughts fled. She loved the comfort of his arms. She raised her face. Her lips met his.

The kiss deepened, and the embrace became tighter. She felt she had always kissed Kyle this way. When the kiss ended, she looked at Kyle with wonder. She didn't know what to say because she felt so strange. She could never make him understand it. She didn't understand it herself. How could she tell him she had kissed him before, in some other time and place?

Cassie gave a shuddering sigh and stepped away from him.

"It's time for me to go home," she said.

Kyle frowned, showing his frustration at Cassie's behavior. He wanted an explanation.

"Cassie—"

"I don't want to talk," she said. "It's me, not you. I can't explain."

"I'll walk you home," Kyle said, ignoring Cassie's "no."

As they walked along, Cassie berated herself. Kyle must think she was a Victorian prude to pull away from such a wonderful kiss. She had loved it and wanted him to keep on kissing her. Only—only—that strange feeling of familiarity had come. It bewildered her. Of course, Kyle wasn't a man from another world, or another time period. It was a mystery, and she wished the sensation hadn't happened.

But I've kissed this man before, she said to herself.

Of course, a few days ago, came back the answer.

No, a long time ago…

The thought kept coming back to her. She kept pushing it away. It was a relief to arrive at her doorstep.

As he walked beside Cassie, Kyle was troubled. At first, he was annoyed she had such an adverse reaction to his kiss. He could have sworn she invited it by raising her face to him. He wanted to kiss her again after the last one. Today's kiss had more than met his expectation.

They arrived at her apartment.

Before she could go inside, Kyle brushed his lips against hers, drinking in her sweetness. He needed this and wouldn't be denied.

"See you at the parade tomorrow," he said with a big grin. He walked away, leaving her speechless.

Chapter 7

Thinking back on her day, this Fourth of July, Cassie breathed a sigh of deep satisfaction. She and Kyle had been together all day. He had enjoyed it as much as she had.

The parade included the American Legion, the Scouts, the school, the churches and, of course, the noisy fire engines. What the participants lacked in artistic endeavor, they made up for in enthusiasm.

At the Native American booth at the craft fair, she bought Kyle a turquoise necklace. She accepted a wide silver and turquoise bracelet from him.

"Both of these will bring you much good luck," the Indian vendor promised.

They hadn't scoffed at the prediction as they looked into each other's eyes.

On the antique merry-go-round, Kyle almost caught the ring. When he missed, Cassie laughed at his disappointment.

"We'll come back later and you'll catch the ring then," she teased.

Then Kyle had a hamburger with all the fixings, and she had a hot dog.

"You've mustard on your chin."

He reached over and gathered it on his thumb. Slowly he touched it to her lips.

Her heart jumped in her chest, and she fought the sudden faintness. She hoped Kyle didn't notice his affect on her.

Later, at the band concert, Kyle confessed, "I played trumpet in my military school band."

"I'm sure you were wonderful."

"No," laughed Kyle. "I was terrible because I wouldn't practice. I only lasted a semester, barely getting a passing grade. That was the end of my music aspirations."

After the fireworks they walked slowly to her apartment holding hands. They smiled at each other from time to time.

When they reached her front door, she moved closer to Kyle. He had leaned down and kissed her, his lips lingering on hers.

Had he savored the taste as she had?

Ah, what a day to remember.

"This is a surprise," Kyle said, shaking hands with John Forest on Friday afternoon. "I didn't know you were coming to Spencer. Party business?"

"A fundraiser," John answered. "Also a good chance for a quick visit to see your new house in Hawthorne."

"Great. I'll pick you up at your hotel in two hours. You'll see our beautiful scenery. It's different from the western part of the state."

On the way Kyle told John about his mother's recovery and his future plans.

"So you're going to live in Hawthorne instead of Broderick?" John asked. "If Colleen comes back, what about her?"

Kyle's smile disappeared. "I don't think Colleen is coming back. If she does, Hawthorne will be our home."

"You're still looking for her, aren't you?" John persisted.

"My men are searching, but the trail is cold. I don't have any hope." Kyle's voice became introspective. "When Colleen first left, I thought it was because I had failed to make her happy. Lately, with this renewed search, I've wondered if there was another reason that her letter hinted at. I never paid attention to it."

"Do you still have the note?"

"The agency has it. They thought there was a hidden meaning in it even when I disagreed."

Kyle parked the car in front of Reilly's Drug Store in Hawthorne.

"You'll get a good view of our main business street as well as the Village Square from here. A typical Norman Rockwell place," Kyle said, pride and love shining out of his eyes. "I want you to meet my new friends and soon-to-be neighbors."

John Forest was at his best shaking hands and talking to everyone like a good politician. He finally turned to Kyle and asked, "Didn't you tell me you've met someone special? Where is she?"

"She's probably at my house. Cassie Brown—"

"Brown! Is she related to Colleen?" John's question was sharp.

"No. I know it floored me the first time I heard it."

"Well, it did me, too," confessed his friend.

"I realized it was just a common name. She's been helping me with paint colors and choosing wallpaper. Did I tell you she works for my company? She's project manager of the Tech Department. When I saw her this morning at the office, she told me she would be leaving the sample books for the painter."

After they got out of the car in front of the house, John looked around.

"Great place," he said. "I see why you want to live here. Your family house wasn't particularly warm or homey."

"No, it wasn't," Kyle agreed with a smile. "Ah, here's Cassie."

Cassie stepped out of the front doorway. A startled gasp escaped from her lips. She had planned to be away from the house before Kyle came home. To see him with another man made her feel unsettled.

"Cassie, this is Governor John Forest, my best friend," Kyle said.

Cassie shook hands with him. "I'm pleased to meet you, and welcome you to Hawthorne."

The intent gaze she got from John Forest made her uncomfortable. And she didn't like him from the first moment. She had never fawned over public people, especially politicians. Never wanted to shake their hands or get an autograph. And Governor Forest's hand had been soft and clammy. She resisted the impulse to wipe her hand on the side of her slacks.

She wondered what Kyle saw in him. Couldn't he see how self-important he acted? And mean, vindictive and dangerous. Where did that impression come from? She'd never met the man. She must be reacting to things she had read about the governor and his administration. Cassie couldn't understand herself lately. Many strange feelings and impressions were creeping into her life and coloring what she thought of people, even strangers.

"The sample books are on the kitchen counter," Cassie said to Kyle. She turned to his friend. "I wish you a successful term. I'll leave you two to talk."

With a quick nod in Kyle's direction, she walked away, forcing herself to minimize her limp. She hated feeling John Forest's gaze follow her. She really, really didn't like him. She liked him even less when she overheard the beginning sentence of their conversation as she walked away.

"Too bad such a beautiful woman has a disability," John said.

"She's a lovely woman," Kyle said.

"Yes, she is. But I hope she's only a friend. I still think you shouldn't give up your search for Colleen. As an old friend, I'd like to know what happens with your new search. Let me know how it goes, okay?"

"Let's not talk about Colleen. Come inside and see the house."

The next day Cassie called Dr. Andrews for an appointment.

"I can see you on Tuesday at four," Dr. Andrews said.

She'd like to get the doctor's reaction to her unusual feelings. Kyle was constantly on her mind. Why did his touch and kiss feel so familiar? Why did she long so desperately for him—miss him and want to be with him—to live with him in her—no, his—house? Was it more than emotion?

And what about John Forest?

Why did she have a personal, low opinion of him? As far as she knew, and the media reported, he wasn't in any political trouble. He was Kyle's best friend. She trusted Kyle's judgment. He wouldn't admire a dishonorable man. Yet...yet...Something was there to make her think so. When they were introduced, he looked at her so intently. She could have sworn a look of relief passed over his face after a few minutes.

No, John Forest wasn't a threat to her. He didn't come from her past. But she didn't like or trust him.

Tuesday afternoon Cassie made herself comfortable in the big wing chair in Dr. Andrews' office. It felt like an old friend enclosing her in its velvet arms. She'd spent many hours in it a year ago. Cassie looked at Dr. Andrews. She was seated across from her, relaxed and smiling.

Dr. Andrews nodded her head.

"So much has happened since our last session," Cassie said. She took a deep breath. "I've become friends, close friends with Kyle Chandler, my CEO."

Dr. Andrews' left eyebrow rose slightly.

"He's renovated an old house in Hawthorne and asked me to help him."

Cassie could feel her cheeks flushing. "I've struggled with my feelings about this relationship. He's my employer but, here in the village, it doesn't seem to matter."

Cassie ran her fingers through her hair. She rushed the next words. "That's a problem, but not the one that has me upset. I keep feeling that I've known him before. When he touches me or kisses me, it feels as though he's always done it. And I know it can't be so."

"Your memory recall may not be total," the doctor reminded Cassie. "You can't be certain you haven't met before."

"But, Doctor, he would have said so. I was a stranger from day one to him."

"Perhaps your surgery changed your features," Dr. Andrews suggested.

Though feeling threatened by this line of reasoning, Cassie shook her head.

"No, this is my old face—no change. Something else is bothering me. The other day I met Kyle's best friend, Governor Forest. After only a few words with him, I got this strong feeling that he was a mean, vindictive and dangerous man. Since I'd never met him before, and only seen him on TV, it makes no sense to feel this way. He didn't know me. He looked me over carefully, then turned away and acted as if I wasn't there."

"Same kind of feeling as with Kyle—you knew him before?"

"Yes, but it's impossible."

"Since Governor Forest has been in the news for the last two years, you've accumulated facts about him that may now be the basis for your feeling. Meeting him personally magnifies it."

Cassie nodded her head and felt relieved. Still, she didn't want anything to do with John Forest. There was something unlikable about the man that he hid from Kyle and from everyone around him. Though he was very popular with the press and was known for his charismatic charm, he didn't impress her.

"Since I last saw you, have you remembered anything new about your past?"

"A glimmer, here and there, but so fleeting I can't come up with anything specific. It's so frustrating."

The doctor stood up, bringing the session to an end.

"Give it time. If there is more for you to recall, it'll come eventually."

Cassie waited on the corner for her bus to Hawthorne. Though her session with Dr. Andrews answered some of her concerns, she still had those feelings of an intimate connection with Kyle. She longed to have him touch her, to hold her hand, to kiss her.

Kyle, always, had held her in his warm embrace.

Kyle, always, had laid his arm around her shoulder and hugged her to him.

Kyle, always, had kissed her—

Somehow she knew this. But how?

What if, by some way-out chance, she had known Kyle? Because of her possibly changed face, voice and limp, she wouldn't be familiar to him.

It was a very scary thought.

She didn't want to dwell on it. She knew he was divorced. Why did they breakup? She tried not to show her curiosity about his past nor could she question him about it. She hoped it would casually unfold in their conversation with each other.

A car stopped along the curb beside her. The passenger door swung open.

"Going my way?" Kyle asked.

Blocked by Kyle's car, the bus waited to come into its spot. The driver blew his horn. This was no time for an argument. She quickly slid into the car.

"Hurry," she told Kyle, "you're in the bus stop area."

He gave a chuckle and swiftly drove down the street.

"How did you know I'd be waiting for the 5:30 bus instead of the one at 5:00?" Cassie fastened her seat belt.

"I saw you had signed out, so I took a chance that you'd leave on the last bus. Since I wanted to check on the painters' progress, I thought you wouldn't mind keeping me company."

A warm glow filled Cassie. Dared she think Kyle kept tabs on her? Did he care enough to seek opportunities to be with her? She looked for him everywhere and was happy the days she caught a mere glimpse of him getting into the elevator or walking down the hall. When he saw her and gave her one of his rare smiles, her heart beat quickened with delirious delight.

They reached Hawthorne.

"Let's take a look at what the painters have done." Before she could answer he drove past her apartment to the front door of his house. He hurried around the car to lift her out. He took his time before he put her down, wanting to hold her forever in his arms.

Cassie looked up at him, her lips dangerously uplifted. She knew she wanted him to kiss her. For a moment she saw desire in his eyes. When he withdrew, disappointment filled her.

"Before long, you'll be able to move in. How quickly everything is getting done," Cassie said in a rush.

Kyle smiled. "I'd like to have everything completed by the end of September."

Cassie thought, *I'll be walking without a limp by that time.*

She could even run down the beach with Kyle as before…

Why did she have this fantasy? It upset her, so she hid it from Kyle. She walked to the front door. Kyle opened the door, and they went through the rooms.

"Lovely, absolutely lovely," Cassie exclaimed over the painting. Each room was as it should be. How easily she saw the right furniture in it, making it a cozy home for Kyle. Yet, it wasn't right for him to live in it alone.

Cassie's heart filled with longing. She wanted to be the woman to share this house with Kyle. After all, it had been her house first, at least in her dreams. Helping Kyle make the important decisions for the decorating had made it seem as though it was truly their house. But she made sure she never gave Kyle the slightest hint of her true feelings.

"To celebrate this phase of the renovation, let's take a drive through the valley on Sunday," Kyle said. "I haven't seen this area. You can show me some of the sights."

Cassie smiled. "We can go to Bradley Ledges about fifty miles from here. It's a delightful place of cliffs, trails and beautiful, unexpected waterfalls. I'll fix a picnic lunch. Be sure to wear sneakers as we're going to do a lot of walking."

"Wonderful. Sunday, at eleven."

Chapter 8

An unexpected shower at dawn made the early Sunday morning dreary. Cassie doubted it would be possible to go for their outing.

Then, the clouds and the low fog rolled away, and the sun came out. By eleven o'clock it was a gorgeous summer day with a cloudless blue sky and gentle breezes.

Cassie wore smooth fitting jeans and a pink T-shirt. Worn sneakers and pink striped socks completed the outfit. His appreciative gaze wandered over her. He gave a soft whistle and a chuckle at her blushing reaction. He put the blanket and the picnic basket in the trunk. Then they were on their way.

"Bradley Ledges were formed partly by an old earthquake and erosion at the foot of the Okenook Mountain Range," Cassie explained. "The trail winds for three miles, in and out, of the fissures of rock and cliffs, under overhangs, by delightful waterfalls and through semi-caves. Some places are so narrow," Cassie cautioned, laughingly, to Kyle, "you'll have to hold in your stomach in order to slide through."

In an exaggerated movement, Kyle pulled in his stomach. "No problem."

Cassie's heart pounded. A shock of pleasure filled her. She could look at him all day. He looked like a magnificent body builder, not a CEO behind a desk. She quickly turned and walked to the start of the trail, breaking the spell.

After they started the hike, Kyle's firm hand helped her to get over the slippery rocks of the stream that appeared and disappeared along the way. Some areas were cool but, by and large, the two of them were hot and weary by the time they completed the hike. Kyle took pictures, mostly of Cassie. Other hikers took pictures of the two of them.

"Here's the picnic area," Cassie said. "The trees were planted many years ago by the CCC young men."

"Wasn't it organized during the Depression of the thirties?"

"Civilian Conservation Corps was started by President Roosevelt in 1934 to give employment to young men."

"Quite a program."

"Yes. Most people don't know that many of our parks today are due to the physical labor of those young men."

Cassie opened the basket and spread out the blue striped tablecloth.

"You saw the statue at the entrance—"

"Yes."

"For once, it's a young man in work clothes with an axe instead of a soldier with a gun! I'm glad this park honored the CCC."

Later, Kyle, replete from eating Cassie's lunch of fried chicken, salad and chocolate cake, stretched out on the blanket. She sat cross-legged beside him, weaving a daisy chain crown. The field behind them was white with the flowers. As she bent her head, her black hair brushed against her cheek. She didn't know what a beautiful picture she presented for Kyle's admiring eyes.

"Have you ever had long hair?" he asked. Colleen had had long hair that reached halfway down her back. He had loved touching the silken strands and brushing it for her.

"No. I like my hair short."

Cassie quickly sprang to her feet, the daisies scattering over the blanket. The sudden recall of hearing the nurses in the hospital moaning about the need to cut off her long hair after the accident, upset her. She didn't know why the thought of having long hair should disturb her. Was it because it had been admired by...by whom? Oh, she couldn't remember.

"Your daisies—"

"Never mind."

Kyle reached down and picked up the almost completed crown and the loose flowers.

"Please, finish it," he said. "You were planning to crown me, weren't you?" A grin curved his lips, and a chuckle rumbled out.

Cassie took it from him and laughed. A few twists and the crown was made.

"Bow your head, my brave one, and I will crown you the Forest Knight of the Daisy Kingdom," Cassie commanded.

Kyle knelt on one knee and bowed his head. She placed the crown on his head. Before she could step back, Kyle seized her hands and placed a kiss on the back of each one.

"To you, my Queen, I pledge my devotion," he said. Then, standing, drawing her to him, heart against heart, he kissed her.

A tender, slow kiss that made Cassie tremble with delight. Then he kissed her dimple. His lips slipped over again to her waiting lips. The light pressure deepened. Afterwards, she buried her face on his shoulder, and stilled her racing heart by taking deep breaths.

Kyle held her to him, reluctant to let her go. She made the decision for him by slipping out of his embrace. Walking to the car, she said, "It's getting late. We need to get back."

On the way back to Hawthorne Cassie didn't speak, nor did Kyle. She welcomed the silence, wanting to think about their tender interlude. Was Kyle leading them into a commitment or was it just a casual show of emotion? There had been a series of kisses but no words of love. It was quite frustrating.

Kyle took a narrow country road for a change. The sunset was pink and red and violet, with the sun a red ball. An unusual bank of dark gray clouds, like a long freight train, drifted slowly toward the sun. Cassie wondered when it would blot out the sun. She didn't find out because the road twisted behind a hill, and the sunset was no longer in their sight.

On the side of the road Kyle pointed to the hand printed sign announcing "BARN SALE, ½ mile."

"What do you think is for sale? Tractors, wagons, farm equipment?" Kyle asked, glad to break the silence and get back to mundane topics.

"It'll be like a garage sale only these people have a barn instead of a garage. All kinds of stuff will be there—clothes, books, pots, furniture. It'll be fun to browse."

As it happened, Kyle and Cassie found both were correct. Everything was for sale. Most of the articles were used, and many had things wrong with them.

"Pick up something," Kyle urged Cassie. She nodded and chose a small white vase with roses on the side. Turning it over, she read: Made in Japan. She had a flash of a scene from her childhood.

Her mother was speaking to her. "Look, darling. So many things are now made in Japan instead of in this country." She couldn't remember if her mother disapproved or approved.

"You can buy this vase for me," she told him. "It reminds me of my mother and when I was young."

"Good."

"Now, I'm going to buy you something. You can't refuse, you know," she warned.

Cassie led him to a birdbath made of pitted cement. The pedestal had birds molded around it. On the rim of the top were a bunch of leaves. Moss was imbedded in some of the cracks. It had the charm of an old and beloved object.

"This is perfect for your back garden," Cassie enthused.

Kyle groaned. "Cassie, this must weigh a ton."

Cassie was crestfallen. She knew it was perfect for his garden. She hadn't thought of its weight or how they would transport it.

Kyle quickly walked over to the farmer. Cassie watched from afar. After a few minutes, Kyle came back to her. He was all smiles.

"Mr. Wilson is going to bring it to Hawthorne in his truck."

Cassie's smile was radiant. She wanted to believe he would think of this perfect day—the thrill of their kisses—whenever he looked at the birdbath.

"Where does the birdbath go?" Kyle asked. The farmer delivered it earlier in the week as promised. It now sat by the back steps of the deck.

"There, in that corner, in front of the lilac bushes," Cassie directed.

"Why not in the middle of the lawn? The birds will see it better."

Cassie laughed. "Don't worry, the birds will find it no matter where we put it. Especially now, since it's been so dry."

She walked to a spot.

"Put it here. The birds can easily fly into the bushes if they feel threatened. We can watch them from the deck."

Kyle heard only the word "we." He wanted Cassie to share all experiences in and about this house with him.

"Here, let me help—" Cassie called to Kyle.

"No, I can move the birdbath by myself."

Kyle picked it up and carried it to the spot Cassie indicated. She didn't know it was heavier than he estimated and was happy the distance wasn't any greater. It would have been a severe blow to his ego if he had had to do it in stages. Or, worse yet, dropped it, to have it shatter into a thousand pieces.

This birdbath was special to Cassie, and so it was special to him. It was easy for him to picture her tending it. Who knew, he might even become a knowledgeable bird watcher.

Friday evening, while he strolled from room to room, Kyle whistled. The house was shaping up. The contractor had a September deadline. Cassie's operation was the day after Labor Day. By the end of the month, she would be walking normally into a finished house.

From now until then, he would court her in the old-fashioned, romantic ways—going to the movies, having candle-lit dinners, walks in the moonlight and rides along country roads. All the activities Colleen and he skipped.

Kyle opened the sliding door and walked to the railing of the deck. Ahead was the back garden with the birdbath. The fields went on and on. It was Cassie's favorite view. He had the feeling she was seeing something he couldn't. No amount of questioning dragged it from her. Her little smile and a shake of her head was his only answer.

His sweet and secretive Cassie.

What other secrets did she hide from him? Her life, in Hawthorne, was an open book. Yet, shadows were in her eyes. Every time they drew close, she was the one to draw away.

Kyle's thoughts swung to Colleen and the past.

As with Cassie, Colleen had been one of his employees. She was in Accounts Receivable. He saw her for the first time at the office Christmas party. Someone had put up some mistletoe. Colleen and he had been pushed under it. She had been a real sport and was laughing.

She was beautiful with her dark blue eyes, long black hair and red dress. She looked up at him, and the world stood still. The party disappeared, and everyone in it. The only thing that mattered was for him to kiss those inviting, soft lips.

It was love at first kiss.

A passionate, exciting love swept them into a quick marriage. His mother had been hurt and furious. She always wanted a big church wedding for her only son with a huge reception at the country club.

Instead, he and Colleen had been married quietly at the Rosedell Chapel with only close friends in attendance. Too much in love, they hadn't realized how deeply his mother resented the hasty marriage, blaming Colleen for it.

The first year of the marriage had been happy. In the next four years, reality intruded to push them apart. His mother involved Colleen in her charities. His fight against a merger took all of his energy and time. The erosion of their time together was so gradual he didn't realized how serious it was.

Colleen's cry for help the last day he saw her annoyed him. It didn't seem serious enough for him to rush home. He thought it was the usual disagreement between his mother and his wife, as had happened so many times recently.

He had been wrong. Today he was trying to change, to pay attention to people's feelings, to see forewarnings. Something was bothering Cassie so he would proceed slowly. He had to gain her trust. He, too, had to learn to trust again. He felt he was being given a second chance for happiness. He wasn't going to sabotage it.

Arriving at the stable on Saturday morning Cassie looked down the aisle. Their trail ride over, Gary and Kyle walked down the center aisle. A sudden shyness overcame her. To avoid them, she slipped into an empty horse stall.

Gary had done so much for her. Yet, she felt no romantic feelings for him. Never had her heart beat wildly or her blood run hot in her veins as it did when she was near Kyle.

After a moment, she wished she hadn't hid from them. It was true that eavesdroppers didn't hear good news.

"Your house is getting there," Gary said.

"The contractor's great. I should be in the house in September."

The men stopped in the doorway. She still could hear every word, and she was embarrassed. No way, however, would she make herself known.

"A big house to be living in it alone," Gary commented.

"Not for long. I'm thinking of getting married again."

Cassie's heart felt like a stone.

Kyle, getting married.

He had been home in Broderick for weeks. Time enough to renew or even start a relationship with a woman. Oh, if only she hadn't been such a fool as to hide from the men. This news she didn't want to hear.

Kyle added, "I have to wait until I finish the last phase of my hunt for Colleen. I want closure. Then I'll feel free to propose and go on with my life."

"A strange case, altogether," Gary sympathized. "I always liked

Colleen. It's hard to understand how such a wonderful and compassionate woman would treat you this way. She loved you."

"Yes, we were in love. It was mostly my fault, not Colleen's. Looking back, I can see Mother made things difficult. She never accepted Colleen. From day one she looked down on her because she didn't come from our strata of society." Kyle shook his shoulders. "No use in talking about it. What's done is done. All I can do is finish my search for her."

"Well, good luck."

"Thanks."

The men left the stable.

Cassie waited until she was sure they wouldn't see her leave. Depression descended on her like a fog. All along she hid her love for Kyle. But she hadn't thought another woman would come into Kyle's life. With his handsome good looks and his pleasing personality, she should have known it would happen.

How blind love made one to the reality of life. She had been right to disclaim the touch of his hand and his lips as the start of an amorous beginning. They had been casual actions of a male who responded to a woman's invitation. For she had invited him, had even longed for more.

How hard it was to think the house was lost to her. She had been living in a dream world during the time she helped Kyle. The decisions she made had been what she wanted or liked. She actually never thought of another woman in the house.

Cassie gave a bitter laugh. When the bride came to live there, she would probably change everything. Too bad for Kyle. He was going to be confused. Her choices satisfied him.

"I like what you've chosen. It's what I want, too," he'd said, a warm smile underlining his words.

Later, when Kyle came to get his treat, they were almost gone. His gaze held Cassie captive as he bit into his.

"Umm. Always superlative," he said. "Please go out to dinner with me tonight."

Cassie's eyes widened in surprise. The request had been slipped in so smoothly she wasn't prepared for it.

"Why...I..."

"Just a simple yes will do." Kyle grinned.

"No."

"Why not?" Kyle's tone was sharp.

Kyle waited. He watched Cassie struggle with her thoughts. He sensed she had a reason for her "no," and she didn't want to explain it. He wasn't going to let her get away with it. They had had a wonderful day together going to Bradley Ledges. Tonight he wanted to be with her with soft music in the background and the gentle glow of candles playing upon her beautiful face. To take a stroll in the warm night...even steal a kiss...

"You have to eat, Cassie. Do it with a lonely man." Kyle's smile curved his lips.

Cassie struggled against his charm. Then, she shrugged her shoulders. "I'll come. I can't refuse a plea like that."

Kyle felt he had won a reluctant victory but he didn't mind.

"I'll pick you up at seven. We'll go to the Sharon Springs Inn."

"I like the inn."

Cassie offered Kyle the last cookie.

"Thanks. Two really aren't enough."

"I'll make some special for you—" Cassie stopped. She should never have offered to do so. She suppressed an inner groan. She had to be more careful. First, she accepted his offer to dinner. Now she was baking for him? Much too personal. She'd conveniently forget her offer!

Later, at dinner, their table was in a bow window overlooking a flower garden. Kyle kept the conversation on trivial, everyday topics. It pleased him to see Cassie relax and enjoy herself.

"Come, we have time for a short stroll before I take you home," Kyle insisted.

Cassie laid her hand on his arm. It felt comfortable walking together. A soft breeze ruffled Cassie's hair. Kyle reached over and brushed a strand back behind her ear. The touch sent a current of longing through her. He pulled her closer to his side for the rest of the walk.

It all ended before her apartment door at midnight.

"I enjoyed this evening very much. Thank you," Cassie said. She looked into Kyle's eyes. She had trouble getting enough air into her lungs. Tension charged the moment. Gone was the simple spirit of the dinner. She noticed how close he stood next to her.

How natural to have his arms go around her and hers to circle his neck. To have his lips cover hers.

The first kiss of the evening was lost in the numbers that came after. He kissed her eyes, her cheeks, the tip of her nose. All the time words of endearment were murmured but so softly she couldn't understand them. It was as though to speak them out loud would break the spell. She reveled in the sounds. Finally, with a satisfying sigh, she laid her head over his heart, listening to the rapid beat—knowing she had caused it. It had always been like this. He had held her and kissed her in just this manner.

It shouldn't feel so familiar.

They were strangers who had met only this summer and were kissing good night before her front door in Hawthorne.

"Kyle, we have to stop," Cassie wailed in confusion. She couldn't explain her feelings to Kyle.

Kyle continued to hold her close to him. The despair in Cassie's voice puzzled him. It had been wonderful to be able to kiss her as he wanted to do for many weeks. It finally happened, and he didn't want Cassie to blow it away. So it felt as though they had always kissed in this soul-shattering manner. It was because love had no parameters. The past and the future had become a part of the present. That's why the feeling was there. No big mystery.

"Are you feeling as I am?" he asked. His intent gaze held her hostage.

"Perhaps." She tried to pull out of his arms but he held her tightly. Cassie attempted to explain.

"Every time you touch me or kiss me, it feels as though this isn't the first time. As though we've done this before." She stopped and searched for words. "I'm not talking about reincarnation. It's as if we've done this in this lifetime—and we know that's not possible."

Kyle hugged her closer and kissed her again.

"Relax, honey. It's nothing strange or supernatural. We just fit together, and it's all so right." He made her look up at him. "You know I have deep feelings for you, and I want us to be together."

Cassie shook her head slowly. "Much as I want to say yes, I can't. I have some issues in my life that have to be resolved before I can even think of a serious relationship with you or with anyone." She stepped back.

Kyle dropped his arms. It felt as though she had lost the center of her being. She loved Kyle and always would.

And always had…

How, oh, how, did she know this?

Kyle was still standing, looking at her. What was she to do with him? They had had a superb romantic evening. The embrace and the kisses completed it. Suddenly feeling awkward, Cassie knew it was up to her to end it.

Kyle had already unlocked her door, and it swung open. Cassie rose up on her toes and quickly kissed him on the lips. It was a brief kiss, hardly making contact, but still a kiss. She stepped inside and closed the door.

My goodness! Where were her manners? She should have at least said "Good night."

Chapter 9

Kyle waited until he saw the lights go on in the apartment. He didn't know what to think of the strange, sudden ending of what had been a perfect romantic evening. Cassie wasn't acting coy. She had a secret, or secrets, that were keeping them apart. She didn't trust him enough to share them with him.

As far as he knew, she led an ordinary life in the office and here in Hawthorne. The accident had been a traumatic experience. She'd had two years to get over it. Physically, all was well except for the limp. That was going to be corrected in September.

He liked to believe Cassie had feelings for him. Look at the evidence—with his touch, her breath became shallow and a warm flush dyed her cheeks. Her bright smile dazzled and beckoned him. All this encouraged him, but he had been proceeding slowly with Cassie, not wanting to frighten her away.

Colleen and he had had a whirlwind affair with everything happening as rapidly as possible. There was no attempt to slow down and consider what the future would bring. They had to have each other—now!

It had, surprisingly, worked for them or so he had thought. Their early happiness had been complete and satisfying. They were happy to be husband and wife, not missing for a moment, a slow courtship or even a long honeymoon.

Looking back, he saw they paid the price for their sudden happiness and passion. They had never had long conversations and knew little of each other's interests. They had truly never been friends. Lovers, definitely, but never friends. It was no wonder Colleen hadn't come to him, to tell him what was troubling her. She had kept it bottled up inside.

He also didn't discuss his business affairs with her. When the merger problems almost overwhelmed him, he never went to Colleen for comfort or relief. At the time, he concentrated on saving the family business and not on his relationship with his wife. They should have shared their lives and problems with each other.

With Cassie, it was different. They fit together so easily. Talking about everything was easy and pleasant. Their differences of opinion didn't cause anger or annoyance. A laugh sealed a compromise.

The house—without Cassie, he would have given up or had an interior decorator do it for him. The chances were he would have hated the result. Probably had continued to live in his condo in Spencer and used the house in Hawthorne for occasional weekends.

This house was home to him in a way the family mansion in Broderick had never been. When he was growing up, and even after his marriage, he had been content with its formal furnishings and rigid daily routine. They ate in the dining room and changed for dinner every night. He didn't invade the kitchen wing.

Cassie, handing out cookies every Saturday, made him realize he had never seen cookies being baked in his life.

Had Colleen known how to bake cookies or cook? If she had, his mother would have vetoed such activity.

Had Colleen gone along with her mother-in-law's wishes willingly? Or had resentment festered within her, to become so appalling that all she wanted to do was to run away?

And he hadn't had a clue.

How blind he had been about his marriage. He'd never make such a mistake again. He had been wise to move away from Broderick. Here, he lived a new and a much healthier life. He would respect Cassie's need to have him slow down. He'd earn her trust and her love.

On Sunday afternoon Cassie put on her old shorts and blouse and went outdoors. She knelt by the petunias. She carefully pulled out the stubborn weeds. This year she knew a flower plant from a weed.

Her hands became grubby with dirt. She loved to touch good old Mother Earth. A fall of hair tickled her cheek. She brushed it away, not caring when her cheek became dirty.

She hummed as she worked. The sun was warm on her back. It felt good after the chill of her apartment.

Last night had been special. The food, the atmosphere, the conversation. Ah, the very best. And the kisses! A smile curved her lips. A sigh of pleasure came from the depths of her being.

It had been so good to be held and kissed. Such a long time since—Cassie's breath caught in her throat. She'd had another flashback and remembered another time when she had been kissed in such a manner.

She had honestly thought she had recalled all of her past up to the time of the accident. More and more, by bits and pieces, events and people were appearing, to prove there was more for her to remember.

Who was the man she had kissed? And what about the man she feared? Had she blocked them both out because she didn't want to remember? That both men, in their own way, had made her unhappy?

Cassie got to her feet. She turned and her dirty face was against the white shirt of Kyle's hard chest. Her dirt-encrusted fingers clutched at his shoulders in order to keep her balance.

Cassie felt her face flush. Perspiration beaded on her forehead. She lifted her lips in invitation at seeing the desire burning deep in his brown eyes.

He kissed her.

"This is the kind of greeting you should always give me," Kyle said. He smiled down at her.

"But I've gotten you all dirty," Cassie said. "Sorry."

"All is forgiven if you'll go to dinner and the movies with me."

Kyle wished he had a camera. Cassie's black hair swung in the light breeze. Dirt streaked across her forehead and cheek but it didn't hide her enticing dimple. In her old clothes she looked about fourteen and adorable. He refrained from kissing her again and again, knowing he had pushed his luck with his hello kiss. She hadn't objected. Had only been concerned about getting his shirt dirty.

"The old black and white film of *Pride and Prejudice* with Greer Garson and Lawrence Olivier is playing at the Rialto. Would you like to see it?"

"Wonderful. It's one of my favorites."

"Is six o'clock too early for you?" he asked.

"I'll be ready."

The Rialto Theatre in Hawthorne had been renovated to its early glory. Everyone in the community had worked hard to bring it about. Freshly made popcorn and candy were sold by the senior high school class in the lobby. At Cassie's request, Kyle and she sat in the balcony. When they shared a carton of popcorn their hands often came together. It felt intimate to touch so in the darkness. Kyle's arm went around her shoulders. She sighed with contentment. More than once Cassie felt Kyle's lips pressed against the top of her head. The tingling under her skin increased, and her toes curled in her shoes. Such touches only made her hungry for more. She wondered what Kyle was feeling.

When they were equally entertained by the actions on the screen, they turned to each other, to smile and laugh. It was special to see the old film together.

The evening ended with ice cream sundaes at the Reilly Drug Store. Its ornate soda fountain had been installed in 1903. The store was crowded with those who had attended the movie. Kyle and Cassie were greeted with smiles.

"Did you enjoy the movie?" Agatha Dixon asked them, an impish smile on her lips.

Cassie's face turned pink but Kyle only laughed. He led her to a booth.

"Ummm," Kyle said as he dipped his spoon into his huge hot fudge sundae. "Almost as good as your cookies."

"Better." Cassie scooped the hot fudge off the side.

When they finished, they walked to her apartment, holding hands. At the door, he kissed her good night. One kiss, only, a touching of hungry lips which craved more. They looked long into each other's eyes—a little flame leaping between their souls.

Kyle stepped back. "Dream of me, darling," he whispered and left abruptly.

Cassie watched him walk out of sight.

Darling.

If only she could order her dream world to become true.

A week later, on Friday morning, Cassie saw Kyle stride into the lobby of the office building and head for the elevators. Her heart raced like a runaway train. He didn't see her standing by the newspaper stand.

Today, he was her employer. A different person from the man who held her in his arms and kissed her. In Hawthorne, it was easy to forget Kyle was CEO of Chandler Corporation. To forget he came from wealth and power. To not think of his mother who probably wouldn't accept C. Cassandra Brown.

Cassie frowned. Why did she put that letter C before her name? She recalled that she had also done so on her application for various papers and licenses. It had seemed so right that she hadn't thought about it until today. Oh, well, like so many things, it meant something in her past that would have to be revealed.

Before the elevator door closed, Kyle looked in the direction of the newsstand. His gaze locked on hers. His face lit up. He smiled at her before the door closed.

Happiness spread through Cassie. She felt as though she could soar to the vaulted ceiling of the lobby. This could well be the only glimpse she could have of him today; she must savor the moment.

Throughout the day, Cassie found herself smiling because of the chance encounter with Kyle. If her fellow workers knew of her double life, how surprised and shocked they would be. Here, she was just an employee and not attractive to men, especially when they noticed the limp.

The limp was there by choice and not a permanent disability. She was happy she had decided to have the operation. For Kyle, she wanted to be whole and normal. Although she didn't think it mattered to him, it did matter to her. She realized that she hadn't been able to do many things that would soon be possible. Horseback riding with Kyle was the one she looked forward to doing. These thoughts made the afternoon fly.

Kyle, also, was thinking of Cassie. He had to make sure everything would go smoothly with her operation.

He reached for the phone and called Gary Madison.

Chapter 10

"You've scheduled Cassie with Dr. Endicott to have her operation after Labor Day," Kyle said. "Because of family experience, I know Hawthorne Hospital is great. However, is there anything the operating facilities need to meet any emergency? Whatever you need, I'll pay for it. Anonymously, of course."

"That's very generous—"

"No, absolutely self-serving! No kudos for me, pal. Just do it for me and Cassie. That others will later benefit is also good."

"You and Cassie?"

"I love Cassie," Kyle said. He paused. "But I don't know where I stand with her. She's as illusive as quicksilver at times. She also has a secret side. Something holds her back from expressing her feelings or telling me what is bothering her. Do you know of anything?"

"Sorry, I can't help you. The amnesia was temporary. To have plastic surgery was traumatic, but she guided me with the pictures."

Gary paused. He seemed to be searching for the right words. "Yet, when the final bandages came off, for a few moments, I got the impression she was surprised. Then she was so delighted with the result I knew I was wrong. Yet, I can't help but wonder what goes on in that beautiful head."

Kyle gave a laugh. "Cassie will look at me with those wide blue eyes. Then her dimple will appear, and I'm lost. I'll believe anything she wants me to believe. But the next minute, the blue will darken with a shadow, and I know she'd thought of something she has no intention of sharing with me."

"I know what you mean. Can't help you there. When my wife was alive she, too, was a mystery to me at times."

"Order that medical equipment, okay?"

After Kyle hung up the phone, his fingers tapped a quick drumbeat on the table. Thoughts about Cassie's operation upset him. He didn't want her to suffer pain. Yet, it was inevitable that she would.

The plastic surgery on her face had to have been especially stressful. She probably worried about how it would turn out. What a relief it must have been to see the perfect job Gary had done.

A new, old face.

One that looked the same as before.

The only things Gary hadn't needed to work on were the color of her eyes and the dimple in her undamaged cheek. A computerized picture, with Cassie's help, had guided Gary. The result was beautiful.

Kyle realized Cassie didn't see herself as a beauty. Her hair was cut in an ordinary style, no make-up enhanced her eyes or put a blush on her smooth cheeks. Her clothes—well, he wished he could take her to the best stores in the city. In all, she attracted no attention to herself. He wanted to make some changes, to bring out her potential for all to see. He hoped she wouldn't be too stubborn.

The following Saturday afternoon Cassie met Kyle at his house. It had been a difficult week at work. She was tired. A sudden shower made it dark and dreary. Kyle clicked on the lights to dispel the shadows. On the kitchen counter were the large books with carpet square samples.

"I need help," Kyle said. He smiled at her.

Cassie leaned against the counter. She didn't smile back at him. She was puzzled. If Kyle was getting married, his "intended" should be here picking out the carpet. Why was he asking her? Or was he the kind of man who expected his wife to agree meekly with all his decisions? That he would present her with a ready-made house, and she would be happy in it because he said so?

Cassie frowned at Kyle. She realized she had been seeing only one side of him. She had ignored his dictatorial ways. As a husband, he could be hard to live with.

Still, he did need help in the renovations of his house. And there had been no engagement announcement. Perhaps she had read too much into what she overheard in the stable. Besides, she couldn't stop fantasizing that this was her house, made to her specifications and wishes.

"What's the matter? Why are you frowning at me? I only made a simple request."

"Shouldn't someone else in your life help you?" she asked.

Kyle's eyebrow rose. "Someone else? Like my mother?"

Cassie laughed. "No, I guess not."

Making the decisions took longer than Kyle anticipated. Not that he objected. The longer it took, the more time he spent with Cassie. The colors she selected were fine with him. He sometimes objected only to make her argue with him. He loved to see her eyebrows draw together and her eyes narrow in concentration.

He hadn't known there were so many tints and colors and textures. Or designs, piles and velvets. Or indoor or outdoors! And what about the padding? Without Cassie, he would have thrown up his hands in defeat.

"When do you think everything will be finished?" Cassie asked.

"By the end of September." Kyle gave a chuckle. "Of course, only after we choose the furniture. Then, I'll be able to move in."

Cassie laughed. "It never ends! What about your condo in Spencer?"

"I'll keep it in case I have to work overtime and for company purposes. You'll like it. I'll take you to see it." He grinned. "And maybe make some suggestions on how to make it look more like a home?"

Cassie gave a little laugh. "That's for the future. Right now, let's get this house done first." She spread her hands wide.

"Although many people today want wall-to-wall carpeting, you shouldn't have it everywhere. You have wonderful oak floors, begging to be seen. Have an area rug in the living room and in the dining room." She wandered out into the hall and looked at the staircase.

It was beautiful. Wide steps with a carved banister. It turned gracefully to a landing before reaching the top. A stained glass oval window was at the wide landing. A perfect place to have a window seat built so one could curl up with a book on the plump red-velvet cushions.

"A deep red carpet on these stairs."

"Sounds good to me," Kyle agreed, looking more at Cassie than at the stairs. The delight and the interest in her eyes was a joy to behold. He wondered if she had any inkling that this was going to be her house. She intimated often that she was just a friend helping an inexperienced male.

"In the kitchen and bathroom, tile floors would be more practical."

"This is going to take forever to decide," Kyle complained. "Besides, it's time to have some dinner. We'll continue tomorrow."

He closed the sample books and steered Cassie to the door. He was glad she didn't protest. He wanted to spend the rest of the evening in her company. A long dinner at the Sharon Springs Inn and a walk home were in his plans.

It happened.

Even an unexpected, satisfying, good night kiss.

Sunday afternoon, Cassie tried to make Kyle make his own choices.

"This is your house."

She made oblique suggestions about what another woman might like. He ignored them. Cassie again saw Kyle's arrogant side. True, he let her choose. Still it was at his command. Her love for him made it difficult for her to see any of his faults. However, these were things to reconcile if a relationship was to work. No wonder it was good not to rush into a marriage or even an affair. In her case, differences in personality and habits were enough to consider without it being complicated with her doubts about what she still had to remember.

Kyle again said, "Whatever you choose is fine with me. Of course, at a later date, some changes can be made."

Cassie shook her head. Money meant nothing to him. Change wall-to-wall carpeting at a whim? Sure. After he married, it was probably going to be done. She wondered how soon the wedding would take place. Social weddings took months to plan. She estimated Kyle would live with her choices only until next March—or even June.

That night, after a delicious meal and waiting for the dessert, Kyle asked, "Is everything all set for your operation?"

"I talked to Gary yesterday. There's new surgical equipment. The hospital has a generous, anonymous donor. How fortunate for Hawthorne—first to have a wonderful staff and, now, the latest in equipment."

"Since you refused to go to Spencer, this makes me feel easier about your operation."

When Kyle reached over to take her hand into his, Cassie's fears of the operation vanished. She knew he'd be at her side. How had she survived without him two years ago?

"I like Dr. Endicott and feel confident about his ability." Cassie gave a nervous little laugh. "Of course, I'm not looking forward to pain, but it's only for a few days. I can handle that."

"I wish I could do it for you," Kyle said. When his mother had her attack, it had been difficult to experience. This would be worse.

"One thing I learned," Cassie said. "No morphine drips after the operation."

"Why? Aren't they affective?"

"Ah, yes. I remember the first time I had it. The nurse said, 'Touch the button whenever you feel pain.' It was wonderful. I floated away. I felt free to give myself a dose when it hurt. Then I realized I was losing touch with reality. Like I was on another plane of existence."

Cassie shrugged her shoulders. "I found I didn't want to have this happen to me. In addition to disorientation, my stomach became upset, and my head throbbed. I decided, then and there, a little pain was something I could handle."

"I'll have to talk to Dr. Endicott—"

"No, let me do it my way."

If she didn't watch out, Kyle could take over her life, Cassie thought. It was very nice to have some tender loving care. But, how difficult it was to keep a balance between two people. After being on her own for two years, she realized she had become independent. She liked it that way.

"It's hard to believe summer is almost over," Kyle said. "So much was done on my house in a short time. I'm beginning to feel like Hawthorne is a magical place, and we are under a spell." Kyle laughed. "Don't worry. I'm not losing my mind. I've been happier this summer than I've been for a long time. It makes me say strange things."

"I'm glad you feel this way because my time in Hawthorne also has been special," Cassie said. "When I think of what goes on in the rest of the world, we are especially blessed."

"I've made an early appointment tomorrow so I'm driving back to Spencer tonight. Otherwise, I could have given you a ride to work tomorrow."

"I wouldn't go with you, at any rate. I don't want you to drive me home, either."

It bothered her to have Kyle give her a ride. It was pure luck that the news hadn't reached her department. Office gossip wasn't particularly nice or correct. She was surprised Kyle—well, no—Kyle wouldn't think anything he did was incorrect or anyone's business.

"Cassie, don't worry your little head about a simple lift to or from the office. I'll give you a ride whenever it works for us."

He stood up. "Let's get you home."

The lazy, hazy days of August passed.

Labor Day weekend was celebrated as a farewell to summer. Family picnics and reunions abounded.

Kyle went home to Broderick to spend the time with his mother. His mother and Aunt Mary had changed their earlier plans and were departing for Europe the day after Labor Day.

Kyle breathed a sigh of relief. He wanted to be in Hawthorne for Cassie's operation and her recovery. He looked forward to seeing her walk without the limp.

At breakfast Monday morning, Kyle said, "Mother, I'm going to leave a little early. I want to beat the traffic."

"It's been wonderful having you home," she said. "I wish you hadn't moved to Hawthorne. I miss you."

Kyle got up and came to her. He gave her a hug and kissed her.

"I've missed you, too. After you come back from your trip, you'll have to come and visit in my new house. I think you'll approve of it. Cassie has helped—"

"Cassie? Who is she?"

Kyle took a seat by his mother and took her hand. He had to tell her now.

"Cassie Brown—"

His mother interrupted. "Brown! That was Colleen's maiden name. Is she a relative?"

Kyle shook his head. "No. Definitely, not. Brown is just a common name. I had the same reaction when I heard it, but Cassie doesn't even look like Colleen. She lives in Hawthorne and also works for me. I want you to meet her."

Since his mother's eyes narrowed, and a frown furrowed her brow, he waited for her to express her feelings. She didn't like surprises, and this one was a big one. He had kept Cassie a secret from her. She had every right to be displeased with him.

Her quiet question surprised him. "When will I get to meet this mysterious woman?"

"When you get back. I want this to happen as soon as possible. Cassie is—well, you'll see for yourself," Kyle ended lamely.

His mother gave him a shrewd look. "Perhaps. Unfortunately, we haven't time to do so now. I'll get my questions answered after I return from my trip. Just promise you won't do anything rash before I get back." She reached over and squeezed his hand. "Now, you run along. Be careful in all that traffic."

"Have a wonderful trip." Kyle gave his mother a hug and kissed her. "Take care. I love you."

As Kyle drove back to Hawthorne, he puzzled over his mother's mild reaction to his news about Cassie. Had she changed because of the fiasco they both made over his first marriage? Or had her heart problem made her realize how short life could be? Whatever the reason, he was glad there had been no confrontation.

When he arrived in Hawthorne at three o'clock, Cassie wasn't at her apartment.

"She's gone for a walk," Agatha Dixon said. "She went in the direction of your house."

Kyle drove to his house and parked the car in front. He walked to the back of the house.

Chapter 11

"Hello."

Cassie gave a little cry. She sat on the top step of the deck, looking at the birds splashing in the birdbath. She had been feeling abandoned. Now, joy rushed through her. Kyle was back, and all was right with her world.

She smiled up at Kyle and patted the step beside her. He sat close to her. He threw his arm around her shoulder. Cassie drew closer to him.

"Getting nervous about tomorrow?" he asked.

Cassie nodded. "I didn't think I would be, but I am. Not that I've lost confidence in Dr. Endicott's ability. It's just the idea of being in the hospital again. I keep remembering how it was after the accident. It seemed to go on and on."

"How long will you be in?"

"Only four or five days. Probably a week in convalescent care. Crutches, a walker and therapy. Then, I'm home free."

"Since you have to be at the hospital by 6:30, I'll pick you up at six."

"You don't have to."

"Yes, I do. Now I want to take you to an early dinner so you can get some rest." He reminded her, "No food or drink after midnight."

"I know, I know."

After Cassie went into surgery, Kyle stood before the window in the small waiting room. It looked out on an attractive courtyard bordered with impatiens, geraniums and petunias—a riot of color. White wrought-iron benches were nestled near the dark green bushes. A robin hopped down the flagstone walk.

Kyle concentrated on the peaceful view. He tried not to think of all the things that could go wrong. Since last night, he had been over the list a number of times.

Several months ago he hoped Cassie would have an operation. An easy decision, surely. He didn't think of what it would do to his emotional state. Today, he almost wished she hadn't decided on it. Almost.

He had loved to watch Colleen walk, with her back straight and her hips swinging seductively.

Cassie's walk had been awkward, and the limp threw her body out of line. Surely, it caused discomfort, at the very least. Then, too, she couldn't go horseback riding. He wanted to gallop across the green hills with her beside him. This desire consumed him.

He realized time was relative. This morning, it had slowed to a slow, slow walk. Had only ten minutes gone by? It felt like an hour to Kyle. There were no other relatives waiting, none to keep him company.

He had already filled Cassie's room with roses of all colors. However, a special bouquet by her bed contained flowers from his house. He knew she would recognize them and that he picked them himself.

Cassie was propped up against the pillows. Focusing was a problem. The outlines of Kyle's face blurred.

"You're here," she whispered.

"I told you I would be." He took her hand in his. "Can I get you anything?"

"No, thank you." Cassie's eyes closed and she fell asleep once again.

Kyle made himself as comfortable as he could in the chair by the side of her bed and looked at her. Long lashes fanned her pale cheeks. Something about the way her black hair spread on the pillow was familiar—as was the way she always pushed it away from her face.

As though he often had watched her when she slept…

No!

He had no logical explanation for these thoughts. It must be because she made him think of Colleen.

After all, Colleen had been the love of his life, the first woman to completely captivate and conquer him. It was natural that she would be remembered by him.

John Forest was right. Until the past was laid to rest, their happiness, his and Cassie's, would always have a question hanging over it.

Where is Colleen?

He looked over at Cassie. His heart ached because of the dilemma he found himself in. He loved Cassie. He did, with all his heart. Yet, he also had loved Colleen. Was it possible to have his old love remain? To love two women? He was torn and troubled.

If Colleen were to appear in front of him this minute, what would he do? What would he feel? He really didn't know.

He didn't want to think about it. He desired only to feast his eyes on Cassie and think of his—of their—beautiful house that waited for them.

Cassie stirred, gave a distressed moan, but didn't wake up.

Kyle wished he could do something, anything, to make her feel better. The operation had been a success. The doctors were well pleased. Normal pain and discomfort were to be expected. Kyle didn't like to see her hurting for any reason.

Kyle looked around the room. Had he gone overboard with his flowers? He grinned. Had he ordered all these?

The bouquet from the garden, and sort of arranged, looked simple compared to the elaborate displays from the Spencer Florist. He hoped Cassie would be pleased.

He slumped down in the chair and put his head back. His gaze rested continually on Cassie. Slowly, his lids drifted down and he slept.

A soft giggle woke him.

Cassie was awake. Her eyes sparkled.

"Who's the patient here?" she asked. "You look like you should be in bed."

"You amaze me. No one would know you had an operation this morning. Here. Let me straighten those pillows behind you."

Kyle's efforts weren't perfect but Cassie didn't criticize. She was happy to have him here, to see his dear face, to laugh at him. When she came out of the various operations last year, no one she knew had been present. She had felt lonely and frightened.

Cassie looked up. Kyle bent down and gave her a whisper of a kiss. So sweet and gentle, as though afraid his touch might hurt her.

They smiled at each other.

He took her hand in his. Her gaze shifted to the bedside cabinet.

"The flowers!" she cried. "You picked the flowers from our garden! How wonderful. They're perfect."

Cassie's "our garden" filled Kyle with joy.

When the nurse came in, he said, "I'll leave now and let you rest."

He kissed her—and left behind a bemused woman who paid no attention to the ministrations of the nurse.

A week after the operation, Cassie was dressed, sitting in a chair and waiting to leave. Her next stop was Jackson Care Center in Spencer. Her stay would depend on her recovery. Cassie was determined it would be short.

"Your Camaro awaits," Kyle said as he pushed the wheelchair to Cassie. He had placed a red blanket in it. The word Camaro was woven into it.

"Oh, Kyle," Cassie laughed. "Now I won't mind bowing to hospital regulations. You can do the honors."

Cassie took the step necessary to swing from the chair to the wheelchair. She waved to the nurse.

"Thanks, Rose, for all you did for me."

"Wish all my patients were as good as you," she answered. "Get on with you. Go in your royal chariot with your noble prince!"

With much laughter and fond farewells, Cassie left, her arms full of flowers.

During Cassie's stay at the Center, her every effort had been made easier by Kyle's loving attention. Sometimes the physical therapy was so hard and painful, she wanted to give up.

"Come on, you can do it," he encouraged her and squeezed her hand.

"Just two more steps…"

She did it.

Two weeks later Cassie walked slowly out of the center, straight and proud. Kyle wished he had had a red carpet laid down and a blare of trumpets to celebrate the occasion.

She smiled brightly and grasped his helping hand. She took a deep breath, welcoming the fresh air.

The sun shone brightly, and a delightful breeze rustled the leaves that were already turning yellow, red and orange. Fall, in all its splendor, was almost on them. The nip in the air foretold of winter winds to come. The smell of a bar-b-que steak in the distance made Cassie's stomach groan with desire.

"Hungry?" Kyle asked with a grin.

"Now I am."

"Good. I know where to take you for a quick bite."

They were served immediately at Harvey's Steak House. Cassie was unusually talkative, happy to be out of hospital.

"I can't wait until I can wear my spike heels," she confessed. She thrust her sneaker-shod feet out in front of her.

"Dr. Endicott wanted to make sure I got my sea legs." She shook her head. "As though he didn't know for sure, or he'd never release me. He just doesn't understand how important a pair of high-heeled sandals are to a woman—especially to one who has had to wear clunky shoes for almost two years."

Kyle had a fleeting memory of Colleen's beautiful legs and her sandals. Cassie's legs were as spectacular. He still found it hard to believe Cassie's limp was gone. No longer would her body be thrown off balance, or her foot drag on the pavement.

They didn't linger over their dessert. Cassie had been given orders to rest. Though she was smiling and talking, he could see she was tiring.

After they were on their way, he said, "You're tired. Put your head back and take a nap."

Cassie didn't argue. Her sweet smile made his heart melt. When he glanced down on her, her eyes were closed and her breathing even.

Kyle thought of his house. It was finished. The furniture needed to be bought. Again, Cassie had to do it for him. Before long, he'd point out to her that he had been having only her input in the house for a reason.

He worried, however, that all wasn't going to be easy. For Cassie, all along, had been very reserved. When he saw desire in her eyes, she was quick to look away. Her body might sway toward him for a fraction of a minute, only to be brought under control. How sweet had been their kisses. And they had been few.

The car came to a stop at Cassie's apartment. As though an alarm had sounded, her eyes opened.

"Good, we're here," she said.

Then she saw the group gathered in front of her door, with Agatha and Emily in the fore. There were words of welcome as well as bouquets of flowers and bowls of food.

When Kyle helped her from the car, tears sparkled in Cassie's eyes.

"You people always come through for me," she said. "Thank you so much."

"It was the least we could do," Emily said. "Come in. We'll take care of everything."

"You won't have to cook for at least a week," Agatha added.

After taking care of the food and she was settled in, they left.

Cassie blew everyone a kiss. She entered and closed the door. Too late, she remembered Kyle had been among those she had closed the door on. She quickly opened it.

With a smile on his face, Kyle was leaning against the door frame. "Forget me?" he asked.

Color flooded Cassie's face, and her heartbeat increased. He looked so handsome—her blond Viking. She gestured for him to enter.

Before she could apologize, Kyle pulled her into a tight embrace and kissed her.

It was a hungry kiss—one filled with her love.

No matter how uncertain she was about everything else in her life, she knew she loved Kyle.

She loved Kyle.

If another man appeared from her past, he would have to accept her change of heart. The accident severed the old ties, impossible to retie. Oh, it wouldn't be easy, but it would have to be accepted. The love she had for Kyle was all encompassing and filled her heart. Kyle could never be torn out and thrown away because someone else—a complete stranger—appeared.

Cassie sank into his kiss and his love. She laid her head on Kyle's breast after the kiss. She could hear the thump of his heartbeat accelerate and gloried in her affect on him.

"I'm so glad you're home," he said.

"Me, too."

"No more talking," Kyle laughingly ordered. "Time to show you how I feel." He hugged and kissed her.

Later, Cassie finally asked, "How's the house?"

"All the work's been done on schedule and—"

"Wonderful." She tightened her arms around his neck and kissed him. "I've been imagining everything going wrong and you not telling me because I was in the hospital."

"My contractor had his deadline."

Kyle took Cassie's face between his hands and looked deeply into her eyes.

He kissed her and reluctantly pulled away. "You need to rest now but, will you go to the house for a short time tonight?"

"Yes, oh, yes." Cassie's smile was a delight for him to behold.

"See you at seven, then."

At the house that night, Kyle resisted his first impulse to carry Cassie across the threshold as he had done once before. She would need to be prepared, to cooperate with the deed—like being married to him!

He had carried Colleen into his mother's house. That was the start of the rift between them, little had he known at the time.

His mother's house.

This time, he wasn't making this mistake. Cassie would be entering his house—their house.

As he took Cassie's hand into his, a feeling of disquiet flooded Kyle. Cassie was a woman separate from Colleen. Yet, there was something about the touch of her hand, the way her fingers curled over his, the heat that flowed between them. Now that the limp was gone, the sway of her hips was like Colleen's. No. He had to stop making comparisons. Not that he wanted to make the comparisons; they just happened.

It was important to find Colleen, to bring an end to his past.

He wanted to go forward, to live an entirely new life with his lovely Cassie in their house. A house she had helped to change and decorate according to her wishes and style.

"I'm thrilled. So, let me see the finished product."

Without speaking, Cassie walked from room to room. Her smile was broad. Her soft gasps of pleasure told him how pleased she was with what had been done. The tour ended back in the middle of the empty living room.

"Need furniture, don't we?" Kyle declared. "What do you suggest?"

Cassie was again reminded that Kyle was thinking of getting married. Possibly, someone in Broderick. It wouldn't be right if she were to choose the furniture for the new bride. Furniture that would be replaced because it didn't suit a rich socialite.

Suit? She'd hate all the things Cassie felt were comfortable and homey, not worrying if children romped over it or even spilled food. Children.

She wanted them. Would Kyle's socialite wife want them? Just an heir, and that's all, would be the case. A lonely little boy with no brothers or sisters to play with. It didn't bear imagining. And she wanted Kyle's children—not some other woman! That had been what her own mother-in-law had wanted for her, one child, an heir, only—

The flashback stunned Cassie. A mother-in-law? Was she married? Still?

Her gasp had Kyle beside her in a minute.

"What's wrong? What hurts?" he asked, fearing an unforeseen complication from the operation.

"It's nothing. I just thought of something I had forgotten to do." Kyle looked closely at her. He convinced himself that there was nothing to worry about. "I hope you'll have time to help me—again."

"Shouldn't someone else do the choosing?"

"There's no one but you who can pick out the furniture. You're here, and our tastes are alike." His hand swept around the room. "Look at the house. It's what we both agreed on. Absolutely perfect."

Cassie shrugged her shoulders in defeat.

"We'll go together," Kyle said. He gave her a hug. "But not tonight. Home you go. Forgive me for making such a long first day home."

"It's a beautiful night for September," Cassie said.

A brisk breeze had sprung up from the north, and the star studded night was clear. Before she got into the car, Kyle shrugged out of his jacket and draped it around Cassie's shoulders.

"Wonderful," she said. The jacket was warm from his body heat. The fragrance of his spice aftershave filled her senses. It was as though his arms were around her. She was content to have her hand grasped by his. It felt so familiar and natural to be holding hands—

Cassie quickly put away the disturbing thought. It was just that they were in tune with each other. She still loved to watch Kyle walk and move—

Still?

There, it had happened again. A sudden reference to the past. She wondered if it ever happened to Kyle.

But Kyle had no past life lost in the dark mists of amnesia to haunt him. She had been so sure she had remembered all of her past. Now she knew there was a big segment that she had to recall, and she didn't want to do it.

She was a new person in his life. The other woman in his life was his ex-wife Colleen. Surely there were no similarities between them. Surely, a man didn't choose a replica of his first wife. Colleen had faults or differences that caused them to separate. He wouldn't want to make the same mistake again. One heartbreak, one divorce, was enough. Another to be avoided at all costs.

"What did your first wife look like?" The question blurted from Cassie. "I'm sorry. I shouldn't have asked."

"It's okay. Actually, Colleen's features have blurred with time, and my determination to forget her." He paused. "You see, Colleen left me. We had drawn apart in our marriage. It was my fault that I didn't see how unhappy she had become. Our last argument must have been more than she could take. She literally ran away after that. I tried to find her but she evidently made up her mind not to come back to me. She's been gone since April, two years ago."

"How dreadful for you," Cassie said.

"My friend John has urged me to make one last try at locating Colleen. I'm waiting for my investigator's report."

"You're doing the right thing," Cassie agreed. The date, April, two years ago, buzzed around in her thoughts. Strange, it was about the time of her own accident. Perhaps this was why she felt such a connection to Kyle.

"To answer your question about Colleen," Kyle said, breaking into Cassie's thoughts.

Chapter 12

"Colleen was about your height. She had beautiful long black hair and blue eyes." Kyle gave a little chuckle. "And a dimple in her cheek like yours. There's little about your face which resembles Colleen—notwithstanding the dimple."

Cassie felt herself relaxing with relief. They were two different women. Only a dimple that was similar. Just a coincidence. It happened all the time.

They reached her apartment. Kyle helped her from the car. He unlocked the door and turned to her. He took her face in his hands and looked into her eyes until her lids fluttered shut. His lips met hers. The kiss flowed between them with the sweetness of honey.

When it ended, Cassie sighed. She slowly opened her eyes. A smile curved her lips.

"Thank you for bringing me home and for sharing your house with me," she said.

"My pleasure, always." His finger traced the curve of her smile. His lips followed his finger. He drew her into a closer embrace. Heart against heart, trading love beats.

"Pleasant dreams," he said.

"You, too."

Entering, she leaned against the door. She listened to Kyle's whistle until it died away. Ah, her dreams would be more than just pleasant.

On Tuesday morning Kyle worked at this computer. A few more minutes and the report would be finished. The ringing of the phone broke his concentration.

"Lewis Investigators calling."

At last, some news. A break may have come.

"Tell me."

"We have a good lead," Lewis said.

His operators had questioned a small, secondhand car dealer whom they overlooked before. A dark green Volkswagen had been purchased for cash by a woman who fitted the description of Colleen. The salesman was almost certain, but she kept her head down and had a cap pulled over her ears. Yep, long black hair. He thought she headed east from Broderick. Yep, not on the thruway but Route 20.

"We're going to work our way east on Route 20. Your wife may have stopped to buy gas or stayed at a motel. Hopefully, even after all this time, someone will remember her. Mrs. Chandler is a striking woman and memorable."

Kyle's heartbeat quickened. He liked that Lewis talked of Colleen in the present tense. He, too, thought of her as alive and only avoiding him. He felt confident this break in the case would yield clues to Colleen's whereabouts.

What would they say to each other? How would they act? It was mind-boggling. No use crossing his bridges until he got there. Besides, too many promising leads had fizzled out.

Two years.

Two long, long years. Colleen had had plenty of time to get in touch with him, to come back to him if she still loved him.

Loved him.

Ah, that was the real issue. Hadn't they both sworn their love was the forever kind? He thought she loved him for the five years of their marriage. They had been passionate in their relationship—but passion wasn't love, evidently. Had the passion cooled, leaving nothing but cold ashes?

As the question of what constituted love arose in his mind, depression settled on him like a sudden fog. Kyle swiveled his chair to look out the window.

Love.

What did he know about it? For weeks he had been telling himself he loved Cassie. Because he ached to be with her? Or looked forward to the moment he could just look at her? Or the way his body responded to her?

All of these things were true, but in his heart the emotion she evoked in him was love—a love that put her first in his life, a love that felt as though he would die if she didn't love him. They were one person, not two. They weren't complete apart from each other. At least, these were his feelings.

Cassie. Ah, his quiet, shy Cassie.

No words of love had come from her lips, but the expression in her eyes told him volumes. Every time he touched her, kissed her, was magical. It was hard to put it into words. He treasured the touches in his heart and mind. There the feeling grew each day. He had learned from past experience to nurture the flowering of love in his new life. He'd never do to Cassie what he had done to poor Colleen.

Cassie would share his life. Never would he put his work before her. His mother, also, would have to accept and cherish Cassie for herself. At least Cassie would have a house that she loved.

But disturbing thoughts flooded his mind. Cassie had her secrets. He had been ignoring them. She might love him, but she didn't trust him enough to tell him everything. Trust and love had to go together. He was ready to let her know everything about himself, answer any questions she wanted to ask.

He was afraid to ask Cassie questions. He had asked other people, and kept his ears open to any bits of information about her. Yet, he hadn't asked Cassie definite questions about her life before she came to Hawthorne.

There was the issue of the amnesia, but hadn't she recovered from it? He didn't know; he just assumed it was so. What if Cassie wasn't as truthful and forthcoming as he thought she was? He had been so willing to clothe her in perfection that he could easily not see the truth.

Kyle hit the arms of the chair with force. He realized he hadn't changed. He had believed about Colleen all the things he was feeling for Cassie. Was he doomed to make the same mistakes? No, he refused to believe that. He did understand himself better. He was determined to make his second marriage work in every way. He'd explain himself to Cassie and get her to help him.

If only Lewis and his men would find Colleen. Seeing John Forest's picture on a TV news broadcast reminded him of his promise. Kyle left a message telling him about the lead and the Volkswagen.

"Wish me luck," he said.

During her two weeks of convalescence, Cassie relaxed and took long walks.

What did Kyle think of her? She wanted him to love her as she did him. How strange this business of falling in love was. She looked at a particular man, didn't know anything about him and yet, she fell helplessly, completely, in love with him. She thrilled to his every touch, was over the moon at his kiss and felt she'd die, surely, if he didn't love her, too.

Somehow, there was a connection between them that caused this remarkable love to be born and to flourish with each passing moment. She knew it was true. Perhaps it was due to reincarnation or whatever explanation she might want to give it; it didn't change the fact of their love.

On Tuesday she called her friends at work. From them she learned that the office grapevine hadn't heard of an engagement announcement of the CEO to anyone in Broderick. One of her co-workers, now living in Spencer, had come from Broderick and still received the daily paper. There was, however, lots of information on his mother's social activities and her trip to Europe.

And, the greatest surprise of all to Cassie, was that they were oblivious to the growing attachment between Kyle and his employee. They accepted his purchase of real estate in Hawthorne as interesting but not personal to the life of Cassie Brown.

Kyle received reports from his investigator for four days. The investigation was exhaustive and thorough. And completely discouraging. Each day was the same. No trace. The final report on Thursday was dismal.

"Sorry, no trace of Mrs. Chandler. She wasn't remembered by any gas attendant, nor was the Volkswagen. She hadn't stopped at any motel along the road," Lewis said. "It looks as though she rode straight through to join the thruway at Spencer. Also, from Spencer, she could have gone north to Canada, east to Boston, or south to New York City."

"Then, we should give it up?" Kyle asked.

"I don't know. I'm having second thoughts about the whole case. There's a disturbing fact. All week we've been preceded by someone else asking about Mrs. Chandler. The only good thing, he hadn't gotten any different information than I have." Lewis paused. "Do you know why anyone would be looking for your wife after all this time? In fact, for all I know, maybe from the very beginning, two years ago."

Dismay and disbelief filled Kyle. This news was disturbing. His mother came to mind.

"Let me do some calling, and I'll get back to you," he told Lewis. He called his mother.

"Mother, you have to tell me the truth," he said. "Have you had investigators trying to find Colleen this past week?"

"Finding Colleen? Don't be ridiculous. Why would I do such a thing?"

Indignation and annoyance fairly made the telephone wires sizzle.

Kyle explained the week's useless search and the new information concerning it.

"I'm sorry, son, that you still insist on looking for Colleen. I hope you will now give it up for good."

His mother's feelings hadn't changed. She didn't want Colleen found or back in his life. Who else was involved and why? Along with Lewis, he began to have a disquieting feeling, one that might prove Colleen's disappearance was more than a hurt wife leaving her husband. Only now he recalled the note of panic in his wife's last phone call to his office.

There was one good thing about the week's discouraging search. If someone had wanted to find and hurt Colleen, they hadn't found her two years ago or last week.

Kyle felt helpless and uneasy. A new experience for him. It was more important than ever that Colleen be found—by him.

Unhappiness filled him. All his plans for a new life with Cassie were impossible. The divorce papers meant nothing if Colleen hadn't seen the notice. If she were now found, what would be her reaction?

He needed to tell Cassie these recent developments. No way could he ask her to marry him unless she knew everything.

Once again, on Friday, Cassie and Kyle found their way to his house and sat on the top step of the deck. Sitting in deck chairs would have been more comfortable. However, they chose to continue to sit thus. Hip and thigh against each other, his arm around her shoulders and her head on his chest, listening to the beat of his heart. A healing peace settled on them as they gazed on the lovely hills and fields spread out before them.

"What's wrong?" she asked. "Is there anything I can do to help you?"

Kyle's answer was to draw her into an embrace. When she turned her head toward him, he kissed her hard. It was as though he wanted to possess her, to draw her into himself. It was a very different kiss from those that they had shared before. It spoke of love, desire, and a need to be accepted. It communicated his troubled feelings and asked to be understood.

"I have something to tell you."

"What is it, Kyle?"

Cassie's heartbeat quickened. Though she wanted everything cleared up between them as much as it was possible, she dreaded hearing bad news. Something always held each of them from uttering the final words of love and commitment. With her, it were unknown facts of her life; today, Kyle was going to tell her what his problem was. Would he expect her to do the same? She couldn't. It wasn't the right time for her.

"Please, tell me," she urged.

"After Colleen left me two years ago, I divorced her. I thought it was all over and done with. Since I don't know if she received the divorce papers, I thought I should try to find her and bring closure to the past. Legally, it doesn't matter, but it does to me."

Kyle told about the events of the past weeks.

"Knowing someone else is looking for Colleen is disturbing. It puts another light on everything. I must go on with the investigation. I had hoped to end it, but that isn't possible because of this new twist. You do understand?"

Cassie nodded her head. She was unhappy. Oh, not about his story, but for the feelings of dread and fear that overtook her. Strange how parallel her life was with Kyle's lost Colleen. Were they both afraid for their lives? How was it going to turn out?

Cassie's heart felt heavy. Her dreams and fantasies about a happy life with Kyle spent in his beautiful house were slipping away. Though divorced, Kyle was still tied emotionally to Colleen. She understood his need to find her and to protect her. Perhaps, if he found her, the two would reconcile their differences. After all, what she and Kyle felt for each other was of short duration and mostly unspoken.

Was there a man she herself feared still out there?

Cassie wondered what both of them had witnessed that could be dangerous? Was it the same type of crime? Or damning knowledge to one's marriage or political life? Abuse? Even murder?

Colleen, ex-wife.

Or was Colleen still his love? What truly made love die or disappear from a life? Her flashbacks made her shy from facing the fact that she, Cassie, might have a husband, mother-in-law or a live-in lover waiting and looking for her.

She wanted the past to disappear so that she and Kyle could plan a new life with each other. Why, oh, why had this happened to them? Surely, they were worthy of having happiness in their lives. They didn't need any of this uncertainty to continue, day after day.

"Kyle, I support you. You must find out the truth."

Kyle hugged her closely and kissed her.

"After this problem has been solved, you're the one I want in my life. Never give up on me, please." He gave a wry smile. "It's a good thing your life is so simple and sane."

It was a good thing he didn't know...

Cassie stood up and stretched. While they talked night had descended. A cool breeze made her shiver. Kyle was immediately solicitous. He draped his jacket over her shoulders.

"This will be one of the last evenings we can sit out here. Hard to believe it's the first week of October. We still need to buy furniture, remember?" he asked.

"We'll decide on furniture stores tomorrow afternoon. I have to bake my cookies in the morning. I wouldn't dare miss."

"I hope it's the chocolate ones this time with the two icings," Kyle teased.

"I can make those," Cassie said. It felt good to get away from the troubling matters of the last hour.

The next afternoon, at the stores, Cassie suggested that Kyle buy a minimum of furniture at this time. By the end of the week the purchased furniture was delivered. Kyle insisted Cassie be present while they placed it.

"Umm. Looks nice," Cassie said. "But we forgot something important—curtains and shades for the windows. How could I overlook them?"

Kyle threw up his hands and groaned loudly.

"Since you forgot, it's your job," he said.

"By next week it will be done," Cassie promised, ideas already forming in her thoughts. "You can move in. Not bad, considering you bought a wreck of a place a few months ago."

"Couldn't have done it without you," Kyle said.

It was no surprise to have him kiss her passionately. Ever since the renewed search for Colleen, Cassie had seen a change in Kyle. His eyes often had a tortured look. She could understand the turmoil in his life. She, herself, didn't know what to think or feel. Future plans were avoided. They took it day at a time. That was possible to endure.

"At least you're able to move into the house in time for trick or treat for Halloween," Cassie teased after the windows were done. She had been able to get a friend to do a rush job on them.

"What do you mean?"

"Isn't it done in Broderick?"

"I don't know. What do I do?"

Cassie explained the custom to Kyle.

He gave a laugh. "No wonder it never happened at our house. We and our neighbors are on large estates. No child would be able to get beyond the security gates."

Kyle thought a moment. "So all I need is a big bowl of wrapped candy to give to the kids who come to the door. I can do that."

"There are a few other things to do," Cassie smiled. "It helps to decorate your yard and porch. You have to get into the spirit of Halloween."

"Decorate? Ah, another job for you. I swear, I'm never going to be free of you!" At Cassie's outrage, he quickly said, "Not that I want to. Please, never leave me. My life in Hawthorne is like living on another planet. Only you know what I should do."

"The decorating will be fun." Cassie laughed. "What costume do you want to wear?"

"I have to dress up, too? I have no desire to be someone I'm not, but I remember Colleen loved Halloween parties."

He recalled his Zorro costume with the black mask covering his eyes and the flashing sword he had in his hand.

"You missed so much fun." Cassie shook her head at him. "No more ducking the issue. If you don't pick a costume, I'll do it for you."

She laughed. "I don't think you'd like my silly choice. Would damage your business persona completely."

"Okay, okay. Let's do the decorating first since we only have—how long?"

"This weekend. Although Halloween comes officially on Monday, the Village Board designated Saturday for the official trick or treat, five to seven o'clock. A porch light on tells the kids which house to go to."

"You love this," Kyle said.

"Very much. Last year was my first experience," she said.

"Why was that? Didn't you do it as a child either?"

"My family moved around most of my life. We lived generally in large cities. It's in the small cities and villages you find this custom. At least, such was my experience."

Without warning, a memory surfaced—

Her heart raced and she had trouble breathing.

She had a husband who had dressed up for Halloween. His face was behind a mask.

Oh, what did he look like? What was his name? Would she know him?

Kyle immediately heard her gasp and saw how pale her cheeks became.

"What's wrong? Tell me!"

Cassie quickly made up an answer. "I just recalled a frightening scare I had one Halloween. Funny how the memory took me by surprise—that it could frighten me after all these years." She took his hand. "I'll make sure your costume doesn't scare a single child. Wouldn't you like to be Superman?"

"Good lord, no. Don't misunderstand me—he was a real hero. I'm not. Couldn't I be a clown, instead?"

"We'll see. We still have time to decide."

"What are you going to be?"

"Ah, that's my secret."

Cassie had played with the idea of being a Cinderella with Kyle as her Prince Charming. Why torture herself about a dream that couldn't come true? Especially now that she remembered she was married.

Why did she have to remember this part of her past? If only she could go back to the time before Kyle came into her life—when her memory was imperfect, and she was happy not knowing there was more to remember than she had first recalled. She wanted to get back to the apartment before Kyle could ask any more questions. She welcomed Kyle taking charge.

"Let me drive you home."

Chapter 13

Tuesday afternoon Cassie rushed into Dr. Andrews' office. She had to talk to someone. She no longer thought she could handle everything herself.

Cassie slumped into a comfortable position in her chair opposite Dr. Andrews.

Without preamble, Cassie told her about the renewed search for Kyle's ex-wife and the disturbing fact of another searcher.

"I thought I had gotten over my past fears. Colleen's story has made me afraid once more. What if my fears of a stalker are real and not a figment of a childish nightmare as I had convinced myself was true? Just because I can't remember why I'm in danger or what his face looks like, doesn't mean he's not real. I feel that he's coming closer to finding me. What's happening in Kyle's investigation is stirring up my fears.

"You've been free from fear for some time," Dr. Andrews commented. "Have you remembered anything more about the man?"

"No, but you asked me to remember what I was doing before the feeling. It seems to get worse after I watch state political news."

Cassie continued, "To complicate matters in my life, last week I remembered I was married! I have a husband who dressed in a Halloween costume. Since he wore a mask, I don't know what he looks like. That's all—no other details. It's so frustrating. I didn't have the feeling he was the man I was afraid of. Yet, why hasn't he come for me? At least Mrs. Chandler has her husband searching. Even after two years. It's been that long for me, and yet, no one." Despair wrenched her heart. Was she so worthless that no one cared whether she was dead or alive? It was hard to bear.

"Oh," she cried, "if only I hadn't remembered I was married. If only I could have stayed in my cocoon of ignorance as had been the case these past two years. It is all so unfair."

Dr. Andrews reached over and patted her shoulder.

"All the cards haven't been played. Don't give up, Cassie."

"On top of it all, I feel I love my husband. We have a happy marriage, even if he hasn't come for me. Then, as though I haven't enough complications, I love Kyle Chandler, too. His life is all mixed up also."

"Let some more time pass, Cassie. Things will change for you."

Since her time was up, Cassie rose and walked to the door.

"Thank you. I'll try to stay positive and let things run their course. I'll see you next week."

On the third Sunday in October, Kyle moved officially into his house in Hawthorne. His suitcases were on the porch. The Dixon sisters brought a welcome gift of food.

"You won't want to go grocery shopping today," Emily said.

Gary Madison brought bottles of champagne.

The outpouring of happiness and goodwill moved Kyle deeply. He was accustomed to the remoteness and reserve of the society world of Broderick. It warmed his heart.

"Ah, if you were a bride, you'd get carried over the threshold," Cassie teased. And recalled the day Kyle had carried her over the threshold. Sadly, it could be the only time it happened.

Cassie's comment caused a hoot of laughter. Kyle frowned comically at Gary who looked as though he might try.

"On second thought…"

Gary thumped him on the shoulders and picked up Kyle's suitcases instead.

Kyle unlocked the door, putting out his hand for Cassie to enter with him. The others crowded in.

It took only minutes to bring in the food. Each neighbor brought her specialty. Tasty contributions covered the buffet. House tours were conducted with nods of appreciation at the transformation of the run-down house.

"Cassie deserves the credit," Kyle kept saying.

By four o'clock, the house was empty of guests. In spite of Kyle's protests, Cassie left after them.

"Enjoy your solitude," she said. "Get used to the fact you have finally moved into your own house, your first one."

"But I want you—"

"No, not today." She left quickly before he could change her mind. The house was Kyle's and would never be hers. If only she hadn't remembered she had a husband.

Kyle stood in the middle of the living room and looked around. Pride filled him; a feeling of contentment wrapped around him. Finally, he had his own house, a place to truly call home. Though he missed Cassie, he knew it was better for him to be alone. When the day came for them to marry, it would be time to be together always. Until that happened, he'd force himself to be content to live here, alone.

He unpacked a coffeemaker.

Soon the aroma of coffee filled the kitchen. He poured a cup of coffee, going out to the deck to watch the brilliant red sunset outlining the hills. The birds, flying in lazy circles, were disappearing into the trees. Kyle filled his lungs with the crisp air. After a short time, he slowly went back into the house.

He settled deep in the leather armchair. The stereo was tuned to the top tunes of the nineties. With a sigh, he reached for the phone.

"Lewis, do you have anything to report?" Kyle didn't expect the answer.

"We have something else to work on. The man who sold Mrs. Chandler the VW remembered smiley faces had been painted on the hubcaps. Of course, he said, the hubs were rusted, but it might help to identify the car. We'll check the junk yards."

"That's encouraging." Kyle felt a lift in his depression. "I'll be waiting to hear from you."

At least he would be starting the week on a note of anticipation and hope.

At three o'clock Monday afternoon Kyle called Cassie into his office.

"Since my move to Hawthorne is permanent, you and I will drive back and forth to work together," he said.

His statement took Cassie by surprise. She hadn't considered such an arrangement. She recalled refusing him early in their acquaintance, insisting on taking the bus except for occasional rides to Hawthorne on a Friday afternoon.

She didn't appreciate Kyle's assumption she would be in favor of his order. He hadn't asked her if she wanted to do this. Oh, no. "You and I will" was the command.

"No."

"What? Why not? It's the practical thing to do."

"It'll cause too much talk. I'd hate that. Besides, I'm used to the bus trip. I like it. I can read or just think. It's very restful."

Cassie turned away from Kyle. She walked to the door and threw it open. She had no more to say. Before she could leave, Kyle reached out and closed the door.

"Kyle, don't do this."

"Please come and sit down. I'm sorry if I upset you. But you can see the sense, can't you?" Kyle led her to the chair in front of his desk.

Cassie sank down. Though she had to convince him his suggestion was unwise, his touch played havoc with her resolve.

"You can't make me change my mind. Until you know about

Colleen, you and I will continue as we've been doing. We won't change our lifestyle."

Cassie's voice rang with her conviction. She lifted her chin and gazed steadily at him. She realized she had been giving in to all of Kyle's commands and wishes—drifting easily into the current of his desires. There had to be a change.

Kyle came to her. He put a finger under her chin. He raised her face so he could look into her blue eyes. Her determination persuaded him.

"Okay, we'll do it your way," he said. "For the present," he added, not giving her a complete victory.

"Now that's settled, I'll go back to my work," Cassie said.

Kyle walked her to the door. Before she could open it, he bent down and brushed her lips with his. Cassie rose on her toes, making the kiss deeper and lasting longer. She had been the one to make the decision to slow things down. Already she was regretting it. But it had to be.

She opened the door and slipped out. While going back to her floor, she was amazed that no talk had started about her meetings with Mr. Chandler. She attributed her luck to her reserve and her failure to join in the gossip during the coffee breaks or in the cafeteria. She had always kept silent about her personal life. Her co-workers had been careful to ignore or not look at her limp. She suspected they pitied her. She probably had made them uncomfortable. Their reaction was to pay little attention to her. After the operation, things hadn't changed.

In the past, when she met Kyle in the parking garage, luck was with her. No one saw them.

Since she needed and liked the job, she wanted to keep on working at Chandler Corporation. She had to keep things as they were until she recovered all her memory. She had no one to take care of her and depended on her salary. When she regained all of her memory, she'd contact people from her past. Especially, her husband. A husband who was very strange indeed not to have found her. The answer could be that they were separated and didn't keep in touch anymore.

Or, perhaps her husband didn't care as much for her as Kyle did for his wife. At least knowing how much feeling and concern he had for his first wife, Kyle would also bring all these good attributes into a second marriage. People didn't change, really. Yes, he was a caring man, but he was also dictatorial. It came with his job and his heritage. A woman would have to set him straight in time—ah, hah!

The next night, Cassie called Kyle.

"Don't forget Saturday is trick or treat. You also should get some pumpkins and cornstalks to decorate your walkway and the steps of your porch," she said.

"Where do I get them?" Then he said, "I'll pick you up in fifteen minutes. You can help me buy them."

Cassie gave a laugh. "I knew this was going to happen. After we get the pumpkins, we'll carve faces on them. We'll have time to do it."

Later that evening, under Cassie's supervision, Kyle carved the faces. The first one had the traditional face he had always seen. For the others, after much laughter and experimentation, the faces were comical and different. They'd present a conversation topic for all who viewed them. Kyle liked seeing them light up his walk. The house didn't feel so lonely.

"Have you thought of your costume?" Cassie asked Kyle.

"A, ha, I have," he said with a big smile. "You thought you had me, didn't you?"

"What are you going to be?"

"I'm not telling." Kyle asked her, "What are you going to be?"

"I'm not telling either so it'll be a surprise."

Kyle hugged Cassie, smiling down at her upturned face. After two unhappy years it was great to be able to enjoy life.

"After the end of trick or treat, there's going to be a dance in the high school gym. Would you be interested?" Cassie asked.

"Only if you let me take you."

"Of course. It'll be fun."

Cassie gave up the idea of being Cinderella. She chose to be Minnie Mouse. She laughed at her big shoes and ears. She was going to surprise Kyle because she had been giving him false hints all week about being Cinderella.

After showing her costume to her landladies, Cassie threw a cape over it and walked to Kyle's house. She was going to help him give out his candy. She passed several groups of youngsters starting a little early on their quest for a large supply of treats.

Kyle stood behind the front door, successfully hiding his costume. Cassie threw off her cape. Her big shoes made a noise on his wood floor. Kyle gave a great hoot of laughter. And Cassie joined him, seeing his Mickey Mouse outfit! They were a perfect pair to greet the little treaters who, at that moment, were coming up the walk.

Kyle was glad he had listened to Cassie when she advised him to buy an extra supply of treats. It looked as though every youngster in Hawthorne made a visit to his house that night. The little ones seemed delighted to be greeted by Mickey and Minnie Mouse.

At the Halloween dance Kyle welcomed the chance to hold Cassie in his arms. To be able to hold Cassie all evening was an unexpected and welcome pleasure.

Cassie apologized for treading on his feet. "These big shoes are impossible."

Kyle chuckled.

"You can step on me anytime," he said gallantly, pulling her closer to him and pressing a kiss on her temple.

At the close of the dance, he asked, "What is the next village event I have to look forward to?"

"Thanksgiving, of course."

Kyle was silent. With his mother in Europe, there would be no family dinner for him. He was sorry because it would have been a good time to introduce Cassie to his family.

"What do you do?" he asked.

"Last year I had dinner with my landladies and their family. They have always been so kind to me, including me in their family celebration."

"You're an easy person to do nice things to," Kyle said. He'd like to do it for the rest of his life. If only he could find Colleen. Why did this have to drag on?

"Come, time to take Minnie home."

The day after Halloween, Cassie had her session with Dr. Andrews.

"I don't have anything to report. I'm wasting your time."

Dr. Andrews smiled.

Cassie grinned. "You're right. I want to talk. So far, I've had no new recollection of my past. I still know I have a husband whom I love. I also have the feeling all wasn't well between us—a misunderstanding or an unresolved argument just before the accident. Something tells me that is the reason I was traveling by myself."

Cassie dashed a sudden flow of tears off her cheeks. "I feel as though I've awakened from a two-year sleep. I was content to drift along. Now I have the unsettling recollection of having a husband."

"How does that make you feel?"

"I'm upset and angry. Where is my husband? He didn't come to Hawthorne looking for me."

She turned to Dr. Andrews. "What shall I do? Ask the police to search for him?"

"Can you describe him?"

"No! His face was behind a mask. He was tall and blond, though."

Kyle's face was the only one she was able to bring up. Kyle, who was her new love and not her husband.

Cassie covered her face with her hands. She felt overwhelmed with troubled and disquieting feelings.

"What am I to do?" she asked. "When am I going to remember what my husband looks like?"

"There is a keystone to your arch of complete memory recovery. You still can't or won't identify the man who frightened you. Perhaps, when you can, everything about your husband will come back to you."

"I see." Cassie kept silent. She was preventing herself from remembering.

Some information would have to turn up to unlock her mind, and all her memories would come back.

"I'll go now," Cassie said and stood up. "I can't talk about it anymore."

With troubling thoughts whirling in her head, Cassie walked slowly to the bus corner. She'd be in time to take the last bus back home.

"Cassie," Kyle said behind her.

Startled, Cassie almost dropped her pocketbook as she looked over her shoulder at him.

"Sorry," he said, "I just wanted to take you home with me."

Cassie looked at his smile—one she could never say "no" to.

"Oh, this is perfect. I really need this ride—and you."

It felt good to be honest.

The next morning, Kyle looked out the living room window to the street.

Cassie.

She was taking her morning walk. She often came this way on the weekend.

He hurried out of the house.

"Just the person I was thinking about," he said, his hand reaching out to touch her. "Come, walk around to the back of the house. The view is different with most of the leaves gone."

"We had a lovely fall. I'm sorry to see the end of our Indian summer. Now I'll have to drag out my winter clothes." Cassie buttoned the top button of her jacket as a chilly wind whipped at them.

Kyle put his arm around her and drew her close to him. They stood looking out over the fields to the distant hills. After the next gust of wind, Kyle turned them back to the house.

"Come inside. I have a fire started. I'll even make you a cup of chocolate."

"Sounds wonderful."

Since he drove her home on Tuesday, she had been avoiding Kyle. She had too many troubling thoughts and knew she wasn't good company for anyone. She followed him inside. He guided her to the wing chair to the right of the fireplace.

He dragged a footstool in front of her and sat down. He took her hands in his. His thumb traced circled in her palm.

"Why are you avoiding me?" he asked. "What have I done?"

Cassie clasped his hands tighter, drawing courage from his touch.

"You haven't done anything," she said. "After the accident I thought all of my memory came back. I've been living happily here." She paused and took a deep breath. "However, a new and startling memory has surfaced."

She blurted out, "I have a husband!"

Kyle drew in his breath in shock. The color drained out of his face. This was the worst possible news.

"A husband! Where is he?"

Cassie spread her hands wide in despair. "I don't know. I still haven't recovered all my memory. I don't even remember what he looks like or what his name is or where he is! I remembered him at your house the other night. In the image I had of him, he was wearing a Halloween costume and a mask."

Kyle said, "I remember how strange you looked at that time."

Cassie got up and paced in front of the fire.

"I wish I hadn't remembered him. I'm angry that he hasn't come looking for me. Why hasn't he? Yet, I feel as though we may have had an argument or a separation. Don't you see this is very difficult for me? Everything is on hold until I know more."

Cassie gave a shuddering sob and her tears began to fall. Kyle reached out and drew Cassie into the comfort of his arms.

"Shush, shush," he whispered, his lips against her forehead, his hands moving slowly up and down her back. He drew her even closer to him.

"It's hard," Cassie murmured. "I can't remember the man even though I know I'm married." She gave a shaky laugh. "The face that comes up is yours, Kyle. Isn't that strange?"

The only comfort Kyle could take from her remark was that perhaps she wanted him to be her husband. The whole situation was surreal and unbelievable. He had been so happy, planning to tell Cassie he loved her. He wanted to ask her to be his wife. To have her live in the house she had helped to decorate.

Her explosive revelation shattered his dreams. Two years ago, when he finally acknowledged Colleen was gone, he had felt devastated. He felt even worse today.

He was holding the woman he wanted to share his new life. Somehow, it had to happen, with Cassie being free from past relationships. It could happen. It would take time. He wasn't ready to give up on his dream.

"Tell me all you can remember," Kyle urged.

Cassie kept her head against his chest. She listened to the strong beat of his heart. Oh, how she wanted to stay there forever.

"That's the trouble. I only know I have a husband. Very little else comes back to me. I believe it's true and not a vague something that I can push aside. I seem to remember he's tall and has blond hair. That must be why I keep confusing you with him. You both have the same build and coloring. His face is a blank. I'm sensing some kind of trouble in our marriage that made me very unhappy."

The despair in Cassie's voice rung Kyle's heart. He put his finger under her chin and made her look at him.

Her blue eyes gazed into his. He had looked into eyes like hers many times in the past. They were the same color blue as Colleen's. As Cassie mixed him up with her husband because of his size and coloring, so he did her, with Colleen.

"What advice does Dr. Andrews give?"

"Avoid stress, relax as much as possible. To let the memories come when they will."

Cassie laid her head back on Kyle's chest, staying in his embrace. She'd enjoy the comfort for the last time. After this, she had to distant herself from Kyle, to stay true to her faceless husband, no matter his inaction. Someday he would come, and all would be resolved. She and Kyle—she had no control of this.

Finally, with a sigh, Cassie pulled away from Kyle's precious embrace.

"I have to get back to my apartment."

"Let me go with you."

"No, please, I have to be by myself."

Kyle watched Cassie and his dreams walk away. After he went into the house, he reached for the phone.

"Lewis, have you anything to report?"

Chapter 14

"Motor Vehicle reports the license plates for the VW we've been looking for were turned in," Lewis said.

"What does that mean?"

"The car isn't driven anymore. It probably has been junked. It was old, you know."

"So our last lead is gone," Kyle said. He wanted to hit a wall in frustration. More bad news on this of all days. This news, however, was two-sided. On the one hand, he might never have complete closure on Colleen's disappearance. On the other hand, he had done all he could do to find her. He could close the case, once and for all.

"Lewis, send your final bill. We'll close the investigation. Thanks for your hard work. You and your staff did all they could and I appreciate it."

After he hung up, Kyle walked from one room to another. His house was empty and lonely. It looked as though it would always be that way. His high hopes were dashed today. Even if Cassie's marriage wasn't happy, it could take time to straighten out her former relationship. If it was a love relationship, it was the end for him. Cassie would leave to be with her husband. At least, he wouldn't be tortured by seeing her in the village, to know she could never be his.

A long Sunday stretched before him. He reached for the phone.

"Gary, are you watching the game? Want company?" Kyle asked. "...be right over."

Gary and Kyle walked to the corral fence at the Silver Spur Stable. They leaned on the top rail and watched the spirited horses.

Kyle opened up to his old friend about his love for Cassie. "The problem is she's remembered she has a husband."

"That's a shock. I wondered if she'd recovered all her memory but never this. She struggled to make sure my drawings of her face were right. It's painful to go through the operations. So much so, her emotions suffered from overload. She had to force herself to look at the finished product—to see the impossible had happened. She had her face back."

Gary's voice sank to a whisper. "A beautiful face," he said, "and I did it for her."

"Not only does she have a beautiful face, she's as beautiful inside," Kyle said. Seeing the look on Gary's face, he gave a laugh. "I know you'd expect me to say that!"

"I agree with you," Gary answered. "So all you can do, at this point, is to play the waiting game. Hard thing to do."

"Perhaps something in the newspaper or a big story on TV may jog Cassie's memory. Her therapist has the theory one circumstance is keeping Cassie's memory of her husband from coming back."

"Sounds logical."

"As you said, it's a waiting game. I'm going to give Cassie plenty of space this week so she won't feel pressured by me," Kyle said. "In fact, I'll stay in Spencer at my condo."

"Won't you see her at work?"

"I can arrange not to. Besides, her department is on another floor.

I'd have to go out of my way to see her. She has no idea I've done so in the past." He grinned. "However, one day we met at the elevator—by my efforts—and went down to the lobby together." He laughed. "She ignored me completely. No eye contact, and she moved as far away from me as possible. Of course, that beautiful blush dyed her cheeks so she knew I was there. She's so worried about starting office gossip."

"Ah, love does strange things to men." Gary hit Kyle on his shoulder.

"You said it. I sometimes feel I'm a teenager again with no control over my hormones or my emotions. Other times, it feels as though I've known Cassie forever even though I'm not fully convinced reincarnation is true or possible."

Kyle was silent, thinking how to explain himself. "You know, Gary, that isn't it either—the reincarnation thing. It's more like it's in this lifetime—when I lived in Broderick."

"What? That's not possible."

"You're right. The first time I met Cassie was in May. I never saw her in Broderick that I recall. I sometimes think I'm going a little crazy." Kyle looked at Gary. His friend looked back, curiosity warring with sympathy.

"I've been a doctor for years," Gary said. "I've learned not everything can be explained or understood logically. Most, but not all. So I've no answer for you. Perhaps you'll be lucky and solve the mystery sometime."

"It could happen—if I live long enough. Or I'm smart enough to know the answer when it comes."

Kyle and Gary continued to watch the horses.

"What if Cassie's husband shows up here?"

Gary's question was the one Kyle had avoided thinking about.

"I'd have to be convinced she still loves him and wants to stay married. Then, I'll get out of the picture for good. It'll be hard, but I want her to be happy. Do you think it's possible for a woman to love two men at the same time?"

"No." Gary's answer was quick.

"Why?"

"A person can love more than one person at a time but never in the same way or intensity. You're asking if Cassie can love you as well as her husband. Not in the same way and probably not as you long her to do." Gary didn't look at Kyle. "You want Cassie to love you more than her faceless husband who hasn't come looking for her. His past actions must have a big affect on her feelings. But, Kyle, don't put pressure on her to make a choice at this time."

"Don't worry, I won't. Cassie's happiness comes first." Kyle turned away from the fence and walked to his car.

"I'm going to Spencer now before I do anything rash. I'll call Cassie, and let her know why I left so suddenly."

"Try to relax and give me a call whenever you need to talk."

Gary came to Cassie's apartment late Sunday afternoon.

"Kyle's gone to his condo for the week. He doesn't want to add anymore stress to your life."

"He's so thoughtful." Cassie blinked away sudden tears. "He's told you what happened?"

"Hope you don't resent—"

"Of course not. You've been his longtime friend and mine since the accident. You can understand what we're feeling." Cassie laid her hand on Gary's arm and gave it a squeeze.

"Oh, Gary, my life is a mess. First came the accident, then my frightening amnesia and, lastly, all those operations to give me a face. Most of this year was normal and pleasant and—then—"

"You fell in love."

"Yes, I did. Now I have a husband to whom I want to give Kyle's face. He is tall and blond like Kyle. How much more complicated can things get?"

Cassie paced the floor, running her fingers through her hair.

"How will I feel and act when my husband comes? Will I wish he were Kyle? How can a marriage succeed under these bizarre circumstances? We've been apart for two years! We're not the same people anymore!"

Cassie gave a little groan.

"What is it?" Gary asked, concern in his voice.

"Just, just getting overwhelmed. Please, I'm sorry. I need to be alone."

Gary shook his head. "Are you sure? I hate to leave you when you're so upset."

"No, I'll be all right. I'll call you later."

After Gary left, Cassie leaned against the door for support. She had realized the importance of something she'd said to Gary.

We've been apart for two years.

We're not the same people anymore!

For all she knew, she might even have a new face!

Her husband might not know her even if he fell over her!

Had he already come and not recognized her? This would account for him not claiming her. And she had been resenting him, thinking him unfeeling and not loving her enough to find her. Probably, with her amnesia, she hadn't recognized him either. This could explain things a little.

Suddenly, the feeling of helplessness was as strong this minute as it had been two years ago. How vividly she recalled her terror as she lay helpless in the hospital bed with her head and face in bandages, her body full of pain and her memory gone.

Who was the man who wanted to kill her? Where was he? Just outside her hospital room?

All these questions had filled her that day two years ago. Today, she had other things to worry about. If her face was different, she couldn't begin to imagine how her husband would feel every time he looked at her and saw a stranger. She had to admit that her face was probably different. Oh, not completely, but just enough. What about a picture of herself as his bride? As his lover? Could any marriage withstand such a change? Then he would have to start over. What if he wasn't drawn to her new face no matter that she was beautiful? It might not be the beauty he admired and wanted to look at the first thing in the morning and kiss good night in their marriage bed.

Cassie's head began to throb.

To keep from crying, she laughed at herself.

What a mess.

What to do? Go on. One day at a time until the answers came for all the questions.

And hope and pray for all the powers of the universe to come to her aid.

Cassie missed seeing Kyle all week.

She knew he hadn't made any effort to "accidentally" meet her in the hall or be in the same elevator or leave the lobby together at lunch. Prior to this miserable week, it had been quite a delightful game to have all these things happen. To have so much to look forward to.

No new memories surfaced to bedevil her or to make her happy. She wondered and speculated about her husband. When had he fallen in love with her, and where? How long had they been married? Deliriously happy or a rocky relationship? She was sure she hadn't had a baby or a living child to come home to.

Why hadn't she asked her husband to protect her when she became afraid? What had caused her to run away from him?

Run away.

She had really done that. Stormed out of the house, jumped into the VW and rode on Route 20 until the tractor trailer hit her. Where on Route 20 had she started her flight? No matter how hard she stared at a New York State map, none of the names struck a cord. It could have been Syracuse or as far west as Broderick. Or maybe somewhere in Ohio.

The questions were endless. She wasn't making any headway.

She wondered if Kyle, in the same way, was wracked by questions about his wife Colleen. Men, though, were different. They could departmentalize and get on with the work at hand. Yet, she remembered Kyle's sympathy for her and felt the comfort of his embrace. Whatever she needed, he would give her—if the impossible happened and all problems were solved. Ah, she was a dreamer.

Kyle concentrated on business. He had to or he felt like his head would explode. When he went home to his empty condo, the feelings and questions came flooding back.

Cassie.

Cassie has a husband.

When had she fallen in love with the man? He believed Cassie would marry only for love—as he had hoped it would be with him. How long had she loved her husband and lived with him? And what had caused her to leave him?

She now had been separated from him for two years. Strange, the same length of time as his separation from his wife.

Just a coincidence.

The last report on the VW ended his hunt for a wife who didn't want to be found.

Kyle pushed his hand through his hair and paced back and forth in the room. He had convinced himself Colleen was happily enjoying herself with a changed identity under sunny skies. He hoped she had seen the legal notices of the divorce that had been published in edition after edition all over the country.

Kyle thought of his perfect dream house in Hawthorne. Would he be able to live there by himself, being surrounded every minute, with evidences of Cassie and her choices for his house? Their house?

He didn't want to live there alone. Nor could he conceive of bringing or living there with a woman other than Cassie. If Cassie went out of his life, he would put it on the market. Still the hope lingered, against all logical facts, that Cassie and he would be together.

He was glad he had never brought Cassie to the condo. No memories of her in these rooms.

He looked around. The place looked like a hotel suite. It needed to have the little touches to make it look and feel like a home. As Cassie could do.

It had been hard to stay on the executive floor and not go to Cassie's department for some trumped up excuse. All for the chance to see Cassie or to talk to her casually. It still surprised him no one had picked up on their relationship. Office gossip was rife and well able to take snippets of talk and actions and weave it into a whole inaccurate story. It was as if a cape of invisibility or some such magic had protected them from the gossips.

By Friday afternoon Kyle decided he had given Cassie enough time to come to grips with her problems.

He entered the elevator behind her. He stood silently beside her at the back of the car. When Cassie glanced sideways, pleasure lit up her eyes.

After they arrived at the lobby, he followed Cassie out of the elevator. When she would have headed for the front door, he gripped her elbow. "Please come with me."

Cassie gave a rueful glance from under her lashes before she nodded her head. A happy feeling coursed through her.

After Kyle pressed the button to close the elevator door, she turned to him. His arms went around her. He kissed her like a man hungry for the taste of her lips.

"I've missed you, missed you," he said.

She kissed him back. "It's been hard for me, too, to be away from you."

With a groan he released her. The elevator had reached the garage level and the door opened.

Cassie gave a giggle. "Ah, saved by—whatever!"

"Only until we get to the scenic rest area outside of Spencer," he threatened with a chuckle.

Kyle pulled into the rest area. Ignoring the middle console with its floor gear shifter, he reached over to draw Cassie into an awkward embrace. When the kiss ended, Kyle groaned, "Oh, for the old cars that had a bench seat in the front!"

Cassie laughed, putting her head on his shoulder.

"You have no idea what I've gone through without you," Kyle murmured.

"I've missed you, too. If only I can continue to be Cassie Brown from Hawthorne. I don't want to be another woman with another name who has a husband."

He turned her face to him and kissed her again deeply. Afterwards, he gently pushed Cassie back into her bucket seat.

"We're not going to think or discuss anything but being happy together. This night is for us."

He started the car. A few miles on the way home he pulled into the parking lot of the Washington Restaurant.

Cassie looked at the old colonial, red-brick and timbered building. "I've always wanted to stop here."

"You may have heard George Washington slept here," Kyle said with a twinkle in his eye.

"Goodness, really? If one were to believe every story, our George did a lot of sleeping around!"

Kyle laughed with her.

As soon as they stepped into the interior, Kyle and Cassie were transported back to the Revolutionary War era. The employees were dressed in colonial attire.

The hostess led them to a table to the right of the fireplace.

Cassie sighed with pleasure, her eyes shining as she exchanged looks with Kyle. His eyes were also bright with happiness. She slid her hand toward Kyle who enclosed it in his warm clasp. Her skin tingled, and her spirits sang.

"What do you want to order?" Kyle asked as he looked over the menu.

"Everything sounds delicious. Please order for me." She studied the front of the menu. "I love this picture of Washington. This restaurant isn't missing a trick."

Kyle nodded his head and squeezed her hand. He smiled at the waitress who took their order.

Casual conversation took them through the delicious roast beef dinner. They lingered over their dessert and drank several cups of strong coffee.

"We'll have to come here again," Kyle said as they left.

They were quiet on the rest of the way to Hawthorne. When they arrived Cassie said, "I have to make my cookies for tomorrow. Would you like to watch?"

"Of course—if you make chocolate chip."

"What else?"

Kyle followed her into the tiny kitchen. The size was great when her hip bothered her. She stood in one spot and only turned to get whatever she needed.

Refusing Kyle's help, she mixed the cookie dough.

Kyle welcomed the chance to look at her and admire her graceful movements. Hard for him to remember she had a limp at one time. She was a beauty, from head to toe. Before he knew it, the first patch came out of the oven.

"Here, you taste and tell me how they are." She slid several cookies on a plate and poured Kyle a big glass of milk.

While Cassie smiled and watched, he took a big bite, chewed and swallowed.

"Ummm."

"The stable hands look forward to your cookies," Kyle said. "What a thoughtful person you are."

"Oh, I'm just ordinary—"

"Ah, Cassie, there's nothing ordinary about you. What shall I do when your husband comes for you?"

Anguish filled her eyes.

"I'm so mixed up. One part of me is convinced that, in my other life, I love my husband." She paused, and then she cried, "Hold me tightly. I need the comfort of your arms." She took a breath and let the truth burst out, "I love you! I feel as though I've always loved you."

"I love you, too."

He pulled her close to him. He captured her soft, inviting lips. When the kiss ended, his lips slid to kiss her cheek and the tip of her nose. He came back to her lips, to drink deeply from the fountain of her love.

He loved this woman.

Had loved her always.

He was as ambivalent as Cassie. He was torn between two women, and he couldn't understand it. Cassie and he were two individuals caught up in a relationship that was strange and unique. The one constant was their love for each other.

Tonight they had spoken of their love.

Tonight was a milestone in their lives.

"We'll work this out somehow," he assured her. "Let's be happy together on a day-to-day basis. Let's not worry about events that may never take place. We can't control the future; only today is ours to do with as we will."

Cassie nodded her head, content to stay in his arms, encircled with his love. Kyle slowly dropped his arms and stepped away from her.

"We have to say good night," he said. "Get some sleep and I'll see you after my weekly ride with Gary."

He kissed her once more and left quickly, not looking back.

Cassie fell asleep thinking only of Kyle's love for her.

The next day Cassie took her cookies to the stable. She passed them around and waited for Gary and Kyle to come back.

An hour later, one of the stable hands brought her a message.

"Mr. Chandler had to go to Broderick. He'll call you later."

Cassie felt like bursting into tears. She wanted to see Kyle today, to hear his words of love again. Heaven only knew when she would see him.

She missed his call because it came while she went walking. Cassie went to bed feeling lonely and abandoned. A premonition that something important was going to happen, didn't help matters.

She feared tomorrow would bring unwanted change into her life.

Chapter 15

As befitted her low spirits, a storm came in Sunday morning. She watched the driving gusts of rain against the living room window. The phone rang.

"Oh, Kyle, it's so good to hear your voice."

"Darling, I'm sorry I couldn't see you before I left. Mother was so upset I felt I had to leave immediately."

"Is it her heart?"

"No, thank goodness. John Forest's death upset her. He's been like a member of the family," Kyle explained.

"John Forest? The governor?"

"Yes."

"What happened?"

Kyle told her about John's death in an auto accident. "It's been all over the news."

"I seldom have the TV on during the weekend," Cassie explained. "I'm sorry for your loss."

"I'll be staying with Mother and attend the funeral on Thursday."

"I'll miss you," Cassie said softly.

"Me, too. I'll see you on Friday."

Cassie mused about this turn of events in their lives. To be wrenched apart when they wanted to be together.

John Forest was dead.

A feeling of relief filled her, as though a burden had rolled off her back. She didn't understand it.

Every time there was a news flash about John Forest, Cassie tried to bring up an honest feeling of loss. Kyle claimed him as a dear friend. He and his mother mourned his passing. She remembered her feeling of distaste and dislike the time she met him. That day she thought John Forest was hiding his true nature with a false smile and a hearty manner.

Kyle's mother.

When was she going to meet her? Would they get along? Apprehension crawled up her spine. As with John Forest, she didn't understand her strong feelings about a woman she had never met. Kyle spoke glowingly of his mother's good works and her social causes.

A sudden flashback of her own mother filled her with sorrow and loss. She remembered the last Christmas they were together—the big tree in the corner, the mounds of presents, Sawyer, her fat, calico cat licking his paw—and Mother laughing—

Tears ran down Cassie's cheeks as more of her memory came back. So many happy times together. Her mother, father and sister Ruth were gone, killed in an accident. She was alone in the world.

Then the curtain came down on her past once more.

Cassie pounded the arm of the chair in anger and frustration. The tears continued to fall. She wanted to remember everything about her past. She knew about her parents. Why couldn't she remember her husband and their married life together for how many years and where? Why did he and, apparently, a big chunk of her life, elude her? What was going to be the key to unlock the past to her?

Cassie cried until she was spent. She stopped trying to remember.

She was going to meet Kyle on Friday, not knowing anymore about herself or her husband or about the man she still feared.

No, that wasn't right. She suddenly realized she no longer feared that unknown man. How did this happen? It was not the most important fact in her life. She'd think about it later.

She couldn't have a relationship with her beloved Kyle until she knew all the facts of her married life.

Her husband probably wouldn't recognize her. She had accepted the fact that her face was different in ways she didn't know. Why she had made these changes eluded her. Perhaps her fear had played a part in the transformation. Who understood the workings of the human mind when stressed and fearful?

What would her husband do? Could he fall in love with her if she was a stranger to him? At least with Kyle, he had fallen in love with her with her new face. He would have no trouble always being in love with her as she looked.

Cassie laid back her head on the chair and closed her eyes. She had practically decided against her husband. This was wrong. She had to give them both a chance to reconcile and be happy as they had been. She did feel they had a happy marriage most of the time. It was only at the end things became strained.

Where was he? She didn't even know his name! Oh, she wasn't going to think about it any more. She'd just look forward to seeing Kyle again. And rejoice in her real life here in Hawthorne for whatever time was left to her.

Friday afternoon Kyle waited impatiently for Cassie to come down to the garage level. Earlier he had gone to her floor and made brief eye contact with her. He swelled with happiness at the delight that filled her beautiful eyes. No words needed to be spoken. He had quickly turned to the elevators and left.

Cassie stepped out of the elevator.

"Darling," Kyle cried. She ran into his arms and gloried in his kiss. With his arm around her waist he led her to the car. When he fastened her seat belt, she laughed, "I can do that myself!"

"Yes, but I want to be sure you're safe."

"Kiss me," she answered.

He wasted no time doing so.

On the drive, they held hands or touched or stole a kiss. It didn't matter what they talked about. Laughter came easily. They were together again.

They stopped and had dinner at the George Washington Restaurant. The waitress remembered them and led them to the same table.

"To us," Kyle toasted, his gaze warm. His glass touched hers.

"To us forever," Cassie agreed.

All during dinner Kyle's heart filled with joy and happiness. Being away from Cassie had proved how much he loved and needed her. Her loving gazes and touches of her hand encouraged him to believe everything would work out for them.

"I love you," he said as he again fastened her seat belt.

"And I love you," came Cassie's answer.

After they reached her apartment, Cassie finally brought up the subject for his return to Broderick.

"I'm sorry about your friend's death," Cassie said. "How is your mother?"

"John's death was a shock. We'd been friends since we were in kindergarten. We didn't get together much after John went into politics. He changed, became more cynical and cold. Lately, though, he was friendlier and urged me to find Colleen." Kyle was thoughtful. "It surprised me because Colleen never liked him. In fact, that last day before she ran away, she started to tell me something about John, but then she didn't finish. She was very agitated. To my regret, I didn't listen to her. I cut our conversation short because of a business meeting I had to attend. It was the last time I spoke to her. If only—"

"Stop berating yourself. You had no idea it would be the last time. You had no gift of prophesy. 'If onlys' can fill our lives and make us unhappy."

"You're right. Life goes on and I've found you."

Cassie looked up at Kyle. "But we can do nothing until I recover my memory about my husband. I'm all mixed up about my feelings for him and the state of our marriage. If we had divorced, then he wouldn't look for me."

Kyle held Cassie close to him and ran his fingers over her soft hair. For a startling moment, he had a déjà vu experience of holding Colleen in his arms and touching her black hair. He wrenched his thoughts back to the present. Colleen's hair had been long, hanging down almost to her waist. Cassie's was short. This was crazy. If only he could find Colleen and have closure.

He was in the same predicament as Cassie. So much had to be resolved and settled before they could marry and "live happily ever after."

"Time for me to—" Kyle laughed and began to sing softly the old good night, sweetheart, 'til we meet tomorrow to the very end of the song, holding Cassie close to him and gazing into eyes that were bright with tears.

Kyle's farewell kiss was tender and comforting.

On Saturday afternoon Kyle and Cassie walked away from the village. The sky was a clear blue and a gentle wind rustled the dry leaves on the oak trees. Underfoot, they shuffled through piles of leaves. They laughed and held hands, swinging them back and forth between them. The dirt road meandered through the fields and between clumps of trees.

Kyle had never been this way. He was enjoying their walk. He'd stop to give Cassie a kiss and a hug and then continue walking.

"Have you given up your hunt for Colleen?" Cassie asked.

"Yes, the investigator had one last lead that didn't pan out. It's time to close the case."

Cassie clutched Kyle's arm and gave it a squeeze.

"All of a sudden I've a wonderful feeling everything will be solved. You and I are fated to be together."

They smiled at each other.

They continued to walk.

"Oh, look," Cassie said as she pointed to an auto junk yard almost hidden by a fence. "There's the burned out shell of my VW. I never expected to see it again."

Kyle's first reaction on seeing the burned car was like a blow to his stomach. He imagined Cassie trapped in it. His insides contracted.

"The fire—" He choked out the words.

"They got me out before the fire started. I have so much to be thankful for."

Kyle grabbed her and held her tightly. When Cassie lifted her head up to him, he kissed her eyes, her lips and slid to the elusive dimple.

"I've wanted to kiss you there again and again from the first moment I laid eyes on you," he confessed and kissed her cheek once more.

Cassie leaned back and laughed. This kiss on the dimple—

She gazed into his eyes. Slowly, wonder slid over her face, and her breath caught in her throat. Her heart pounded in her chest. She blinked once, and then a second time, as though to make sure she was seeing right. She reached up and stroked Kyle's cheeks. A light burned in her eyes.

She whispered, "You're my husband."

Kyle smiled at her.

"Not yet, but soon," was his laughing, happy answer.

"No, no! You're my husband. I'm Colleen."

"Don't kid me. You're Cassie Brown. Besides you don't look like Colleen." Kyle's voice was sharp. "No way are you Colleen."

"But I remember everything," she protested.

Over the top of her head, he looked again at the burned VW. His gaze fell to the rusted, blackened hubcaps. It took a moment for his mind to process what his gaze was seeing—smiley faces!

Was it possible?

It couldn't be. No way.

He looked closely at the woman who had made an impossible statement. This was definitely the face of Cassie Brown.

The eyes, the dimple, the color of the hair and how it framed her face—these were similar to Colleen, but other features—the cheekbones, the chin, even the voice— were different from Colleen. He shook his head. It just couldn't be.

"I don't understand. If you're Colleen, why did you have Gary give you a different face?"

"I didn't realize I did." She stopped, trying to find the right words. "I left Broderick because I believed John Forest wanted to kill me. I planned to go to the Spencer condo and call you. I never intended to disappear. The accident happened, and I couldn't remember parts of my life. Only my life before I ever met or married you. My full name is Cassandra Colleen Brown. When I met you, I used Colleen because I never liked Cassandra. I was teased as a child about it."

"That clears things up quite a lot," Kyle said. "But tell me. John— wanted to kill you? Are you sure?" Kyle shook his head in unbelief.

"I didn't think you'd believe me. See, already you're doubting me. No wonder I left!"

She pulled away from Kyle and started to run down the road.

Kyle caught up with her and stopped her flight. "I'm sorry. Please tell me everything. I'm sorry we drifted apart so much that you couldn't come to me so I could protect you. You must forgive me."

She let him pull her into his arms once more.

"Don't ever let me go again," she said.

"I won't." He still couldn't see Colleen when he only saw Cassie! "Tell me what happened. From the beginning. From the night you left Broderick and me."

The words spilled out.

"I had gone to John's apartment to get him to talk at a fundraiser. The door swung open when I knocked. I could see into the hall. John was choking a woman. I froze. After he dropped her, he looked up and saw me. I just ran away. I couldn't believe what I had seen. When nothing came out in the news, I thought it was just an argument."

"Go on."

"Then the accidents kept happening. I got pushed down the stairs and, another time, in front of a bus. My car was run off the road. Finally, I knew I had seen something that would jeopardize John's political career. He wanted me out of the way. I called you—"

"Yes, and I didn't listen. So you left. I'm so sorry."

With a shudder, Colleen stopped talking.

"Please go on," Kyle urged, holding her closer, patting her back and pressing kisses on her forehead.

"It was so frightening to wake up in the hospital and to have amnesia. All I remembered was a man wanted to hurt me."

"What about the plastic surgery on your face?"

"I honestly believed I remembered what I looked like. And I did remember the years before my accident—to a point in time. I just didn't recall the last five years—my marriage and you. I was happy in Hawthorne. I was Cassandra Brown, the woman who fell in love with her employer. He even let her decorate his house—her house." She shook her head. "Evidently, my fear of that unknown man was the keystone that needed to fall. With John's death, the block to my memory was released. I could then see you were my husband! No wonder I was giving Cassie's husband your face!"

She clasped his hands in hers.

"No wonder I always felt I knew you."

"And I, you."

"You don't, by any chance, have a picture of me as Colleen tucked away in your wallet?" she asked. "I'd like to see it."

Kyle rummaged in his wallet. He pulled out a ragged snapshot. "I forgot I had this all this time." He waited for her reaction.

"Oh, my face is different. No wonder you didn't recognize me. The differences aren't great but just enough to mislead."

She continued to look at the picture. She gave a wail. "Who do you love? Colleen? Cassie? What are we going to do? Your mother—"

Kyle chuckled. "We'll have to re-marry. It will be a great shock to her. She'll have a time getting used to your new face. At least we'll be living in Hawthorne. Since her heart attack she's mellowed—at least I like to think so. People will be surprised, but they also will accept the story when we explain. After all, it's a wonderful, fairy-tale ending."

Kyle laughed. He picked her up and swung her around in a circle.

"What a wonderful life I shall live. Two wives and each one claiming all my love." His lips covered hers. "We'll live happily ever after. I shall have to watch what I call you—"

"Just call me your dearest darling forever."

Printed in the United States
84770LV00002BA/164/A